THE TREATMENT

"Are you ready, Bubba?"

Bubba's eyes were closed. Tight. His whole face was clenched in an expression of total rejection and total fear.

"Open your eyes, Bubba," Dr. Ross directed him, gently. *"Open your eyes and see what's out there! It's your fear, and you've got to face it!"*

Shaking, as if he were suffering from chronic pneumonia, Bubba slowly opened his eyes. He stared at the walls around him, and his jaw stiffened in horror. There was no question of his closing his eyes now. He was too frightened.

On the walls, all around him, were dozens of snakes. Sliding and writhing and twisting over each other, rattlesnakes and water moccasins and sidewinders, dry and slithery and flicking their tongues.

LARRY SPIEGEL AND MEL BERGMAN PRESENT
A JOHN HUSTON FILM
PAUL MICHAEL GLASER   SUSAN HOGAN
IN

PHOBIA

STARRING
JOHN COLICOS
EXECUTIVE PRODUCERS
LARRY SPIEGEL & MEL BERGMAN
PRODUCED BY
ZALE MAGDER
DIRECTED BY
JOHN HUSTON
STORY BY
GARY SHERMAN &, RONALD SHUSETT
SCREENPLAY BY
LEW   JIMMY   PETER
LEHMAN, SANGSTER, BELLWOOD

Thomas Luke

PHOBIA

Screenplay by
Lew   Jimmy   Peter
Lehman, Sangster, Bellwood

Based on story by
Gary Sherman & Ronald Shusett

PUBLISHED BY POCKET BOOKS NEW YORK

Another *Original* publication of POCKET BOOKS

POCKET BOOKS, a Simon & Schuster division of
GULF & WESTERN CORPORATION
1230 Avenue of the Americas, New York, N.Y. 10020

ISBN: 0-671-83662-5

First Pocket Books printing September, 1980

10 9 8 7 6 5 4 3 2 1

POCKET and colophon are trademarks of Simon & Schuster.

Printed in the U.S.A.

"If a madman were to come into this
room with a stick in his hand, no
doubt we should pity the state of
his mind; but our primary consider-
ation would be to take care of ourselves. We should knock him down first,
and pity him afterwards."

—Dr. Samuel Johnson, 1776

"The world is no place for the bad,
the stupid, the enervated. Their
duty—it's a fine duty too!—is to
die. The death of the failure! That
is the path . . . by which man goes on to
higher things."

—H. G. Wells, *When the Sleeper
Wakes*

1

IT WAS ONE of those days when sunlight brightens and fades, brightens and fades, like pictures in a forgotten family album. First, a picture of a small red-roofed house just outside of La Canada, a mile or two north of Pasadena, in the cooler foothills of the San Gabriel Mountains. Then, a picture of a father, with short brilliantined hair and wide gray slacks, briskly washing a new Dodge Royal in the driveway. A picture of a mother, slim, with a green spotted headscarf, setting out Saturday lunch on the kitchen table and listening to Duke Ellington on the radio playing *Reflections in D*.

And outside in the back yard, reflected in the breeze-ribbed surface of the swimming pool, two children playing idle games. A little girl of five, with shining brown hair and a too-cute pink bikini. A boy of seven, with thick curly hair and that cross, aggressive frown that seven-year-old boys can walk around with all day.

All around the children, the chirruping of birds, the sudden rustling of leaves and the sunlight that dazzled one minute and died the next.

"Dolly wants to swim," announced the little girl. (You could hardly have heard this, with the wind blowing, and the distant sound of a bulldozer where they were constructing a new supermarket.)

7

"She'll sink, stupid," said the little boy, his arm raised against the glare. He'd been chalking faces on the patio, faces of spacemen and cowboys and clowns. Faces of gangsters, too, which was one of those disturbing not-quite-coincidences that he never forgot.

"She can swim now. She learned."

"She cannot swim. How can she swim? The water always gets in through the holes in her eyes."

"She learned to keep them shut."

"How can she learn if she doesn't have any brains?"

"She does too have brains."

The boy watched his sister for a moment in silence. Then he said, "Okay then, you put her in the pool and you see just how well she swims. Then just see what Daddy says when she sinks right to the bottom, that's all."

(And now, one of those long breathless minutes that are always remembered afterward because they were crowded with trivia, with radio music that was still faintly playing from the open kitchen window, with soapsuds that ran down the curved hood of the car, with the ping of the timer on the cooker and the muted laughter of next door's children. And, in the same minute, for no reason at all except that parents are parents and are wired into the very sound of their children living and breathing, a growing feeling that something, somewhere, has gone very badly wrong.)

The little girl, studiously bent over the pool. The doll, in a sodden pink dress, circling and slowly sinking, with reflections sparkling around it like fragments of broken mirrors. The boy, with his tongue between his teeth, carefully chalking Dick Tracy's hat.

"Dolly's drowning."

Followed by a rippling splash so subdued that the boy hardly heard it, and then a gurgle. So that it was only when the water at his end of the pool began to lap loudly at the blue-painted sides that he looked up and saw his sister's fist snatching and squeezing at the air.

He rose slowly to his feet. It might have been quickly, but in the dreams he had about it afterward, it was always slowly, and stickily, as if time had turned into honey. He ran the length of the pool, and while he was running he saw her face just under the surface, eyes and mouth wide open, just like she was shouting at him, only there was no sound at all.

He knelt by the side of the pool, skinning his knees on the concrete. He reached out, but she was already too far away, and too deep. He could see her sinking to the bottom, her hair waving all around her, her legs strangely dwarfish because of the refracted light. Her skin looked bluish white; her pink bikini had turned gray.

He looked up. His mother was standing at the open kitchen door, wiping her hands on her apron. Her expression was colorless and rigid, as if an artist had asked her to pose like that. *A Tragedy in the Suburbs,* by Andrew Wyeth, in tempera and fear. And there was still that overwhelming silence.

It was only when his father came bursting in through the white-painted side gate that the noise exploded.

"Suzie! My God, Suzie!"

Then his mother screaming, a weird high-pitched sound that would have stopped a dog in its tracks, and the huge splash of his father diving fully clothed into the water, sending drops of water spattering halfway up the creosoted fence.

His father surfaced at last, gasping, thrashing at the water. There were neighbors all around; he couldn't think where they'd come from, and they were helping his father out. He heard a woman saying, "Oh, I don't believe it, I don't believe it," over and over again.

He stood a little way away from the jostling circle of helpers, his hands by his sides, biting his lip, stiff with the knowledge of the one catastrophic fact which none of the adults seemed to want to admit, that Suzie was drowned. The sun went behind a cloud and then reappeared again, uncomfortably dazzling. His father was grunting as he tried to pump the water out of his daughter's lungs. His mother was whimpering, a terrible endless whimper that he could hardly bear to listen to.

He looked across the yard and there was his drawing of Dick Tracy, with the piece of chalk lying beside it where he had left it.

"Is she responding?" someone asked. "Will someone get a mirror please? A mirror—to check if she's breathing. That's right."

"What the hell is keeping them with that ambulance?"

"My God, I didn't hear a thing. Not a thing. He didn't even call out. I just got this feeling and I went to check they were okay. Can you believe that? He didn't even call out."

In the distance, over the grinding echoes of the bulldozers, he heard the wailing of a siren. He couldn't see Suzie for a moment, through all those hairy adult legs, with their white socks and their tennis shoes, but then somebody stood aside and he caught a glimpse of tangled brown hair, already half-dried, and a pale shoulder. He wanted very much to go kneel beside her and tell her how much he loved her, and how sorry he was. He wanted to touch her. But there were too many adults around and he could see how upset his father was already.

He looked down at the pool. The doll, half-submerged, was still circling around, its eyes blinking with every ripple. He carefully fished it out and held it up, so that the water poured out of its eyes.

There was an unexpected silence as the siren died away, and the bulldozers stopped churning, and everybody stopped talking all at once. The only sound was the water trickling out of the upturned doll onto the side of the pool.

His father turned toward him. When he saw what he was doing, his father's face seemed to take on the stunned, questioning look of complete disbelief.

"Your sister is dead," he said, harshly and softly.

The boy didn't know what he was supposed to do. He looked for his mother but he couldn't see her anywhere. He knew his sister was dead. He had known she was dead from the moment he had run along the length of the pool, and seen her shouting at him below the surface, as if she was trying to call goodbye from another dimension.

The last drops of water poured out of the doll.

"How can you stand there doing that when your sister is dead!" screeched his father. And then there was pushing and scrambling, and someone said, "John—I don't think he—" and the morning broke into jagged fragments of voices and faces and snatched images of sunlight and shadow and a wheeled stretcher that was covered with a lemon-yellow blanket.

He spent the rest of the afternoon with neighbors. The sun brightened and faded through the window. They wouldn't let him outside to play, but let him watch television instead. He fell asleep on the chintzy settee halfway through *I Love Lucy,* the one in which Desi Arnaz gets morning sickness in sympathy with Lucy's pregnancy. But he woke in time to hear his father and mother in the hallway outside.

"—gave her something to sleep—you know, just for—"

"—can't tell you how sorry I am—"

"—sudden—"

"—if only he'd called me—that's what I can't under-stand—if only he'd called me—"

Then his father came in, and stood watching him for a long while, knowing that he wasn't really asleep because his closed eyelids were flickering.

"Come on, cowboy," his father said, leaning over him. "It's time to go home."

2

HE HELD UP the chart so that the other doctors could see it. At the far end of the polished table, Dr. Clegg took a pair of horn-rimmed half-glasses out of his breast pocket and raised them in front of his eyes with that kind of squeezed-lemon expression which meant he found the chart just as blurry to understand as it was to see.

But he didn't let Dr. Clegg faze him. He simply gave him a courteous nod, and pointed his pencil to the rising curve on the chart with all the briskness of a man who knows exactly what he's doing.

"This curve is a measure of my patients' progress," he said. "Hours of therapy against empirical improvements. It's been slow, as you can see. A little slower than I first expected. But you have to remember the magnitude of the disorders I've been treating here, and all the associated problems that I have to deal with at the same time.

"Of course, each patient's particular phobia is at the epicenter of his or her condition. But I'm also having to cope with the psychological effects of environmental deprivation, social hostility, drug abuse, alcoholism, institutional withdrawal and you name it.

"Apart from curing them of their irrational fears, I

13

have to be their social worker, their priest, their friend, their analyst and their father. In fact, most of them treat me and regard me as a father above anything else."

"A sort of psychologically qualified Santa Claus," put in Dr. Clegg dryly.

He allowed himself to smile. He knew that Dr. Clegg, for all of his sarcasm, was both fair-minded and friendly. Dr. Clegg simply enjoyed using his white-haired seniority and his poker-faced wit to put his colleagues off balance, to make them defend their therapy work more fiercely, and to make sure that, when they came around the discussion table, they had their reports and their results as tightly sewn up as a brain surgeon's suture.

"The rehabilitation aspect of the work is vital," he told Dr. Clegg. "Apart from conquering their fear of heights, or of water, or of enclosed spaces, my patients must also learn to adapt to the society which has punished them for having those fears. They have to get over their fear of being afraid."

"How far does this go back?" asked Dr. Clegg. "Don't tell me they have to get over their fear of being afraid of being afraid, and so forth."

"They're doing pretty well," he retorted. "It looks like we're going to be able to finish the research in the time allotted, despite the unexpected holdups. In fact, if you check with the chart here, you'll see that most of them are more than seventy percent through their work with me."

There was a murmur of approval from the doctors around the table. He glanced quickly at Dr. Alice Toland, sitting next to Dr. Clegg, and she gave him a small pursed smile and a nod of the head.

"I think Dr. Ross ought to be congratulated," she said.

Only Dr. Clemens refused to look impressed. She

slapped her notepad shut as if she was trying to catch a mouse in it, and then sat with her arms folded. She was a short, peppery-haired woman with a fierce reputation for exact mathematics and speaking her own mind.

"Do you have some difference of opinion to express, Dr. Clemens?" asked Dr. Clegg.

"Yes," said Dr. Clemens sharply, as if it wasn't already obvious. "Not about Dr. Ross's motives, which I'm sure are impeccable, if not saintly, but about his results. I've seen one or two of your patients when they've been returning from your treatment room, Dr. Ross, and all I can say is that if they're seventy percent through now, God help them when they're one hundred percent through."

"What exactly are you trying to suggest?" asked Dr. Ross, trying to keep his voice as flat and as calm as possible. "Are you trying to suggest that—"

"I'm not trying to suggest anything," interrupted Dr. Clemens. "I'm simply expressing the opinion that your patients come out of treatment looking like they've been trampled by buffalo."

Dr. Ross tossed his chart back on the table, paused and carefully licked his lips. Then he said steadily, "They come out that way, Dr. Clemens, because I have to put them through an experience that's ten times more traumatic than being trampled by a few cows. I have to take them right into the raw center of their deepest fears—right to the point where their phobias are rooted —and I have to make them face up to whatever it is they're afraid of."

"Perhaps Santa Claus was a poor comparison," said Dr. Clegg.

Dr. Ross disregarded him. "You know how the Scientologists constantly repeat words until the words lose all their frightening associations—well, that's what I'm doing, except in color and sound and three dimensions. Every time my patients go into my treatment room, they're experiencing their own particular variety of hell —as real as I can possibly make it. They come out shattered—of course they do. But each time they come out, they're a little stronger, and a little less afraid, and the day is soon going to arrive when they're not afraid at all."

"I see," said Dr. Clemens. "And is it unprofessional to ask you how you first conceived that such a treatment might actually work?"

Dr. Ross ran his hand through his thick dark curls. "I've based it on my own personal experience, as a matter of fact. When I was younger, I was afraid of water. I didn't want to learn to swim because of it. And in California, where I was brought up, you can imagine what kind of a handicap that was."

He stood up and walked around to the back of Dr. Clemens's chair. She listened, but her eyes didn't follow him.

"My father was a fine swimmer," said Dr. Ross, "and like most fathers, he wanted me to do everything he did, and do it well. He tried bribing me with a BB gun. He tried persuading me. He even tried shouting at me. But—when none of these things brought me any nearer to swimming—he picked me right up one day and threw me straight in the pool."

"Needless to say you didn't drown," Dr. Clemens interjected.

"Well, you're right." Dr. Ross grinned. "As a matter of fact, I swam, and I kept on swimming. And that's a simplistic but accurate comparison to what I'm doing with my phobia patients. I'm throwing them straight in the pool, so that they can discover for themselves that they can swim."

"You were pretty young when your father did that," said Dr. Clegg. "That must have helped some."

"Of course," agreed Dr. Ross. "With an older person, whose phobia has conditioned their daily living habits for years, you have to take the treatment more slowly. Somebody who's claustrophobic, for instance, has probably spent his whole life avoiding subways and elevators and crowded rooms, and while you can break the basic phobia quite quickly, you still have to tackle all the associated behavior patterns."

Dr. Clemens picked up her copy of Dr. Ross's figures and reports. "I think you've answered my question, Doctor," she said in a precise tone. "And from what I've read of your progress, you seem to be doing remarkably well in a very difficult field of therapy. I'm sorry I was so full frontal with you. *I* think we should congratulate you, too."

Dr. Ross leaned forward. "Thank you," he said, very warmly, and smiled at her as she turned. She nodded in acknowledgment, but didn't smile back.

Dr. Clegg said, "Tell me, Dr. Ross, what's happened to your great buddy Captain Barnes?"

"Barnes? He's quiet at the moment," said Dr. Ross, going back to his chair.

"Did you persuade him to withdraw that complaint to the Prison Parole Board about your using convicted criminals as guinea pigs?"

"I've reassured him that I'm not running a rest home for homicidal maniacs, if that's what you mean. But he's strictly a badge-and-gun man. He finds it hard to believe that phobias exist at all—let alone that they could be responsible for a phobic's criminal actions. Still—he's been quiet lately. I think he's prepared to wait and see."

Dr. Clegg folded up his spectacles and tucked them back in his breast pocket. "Dr. Ross," he said, "I believe you've met this Ethics Committee's concern for the progress and welfare of your research subjects."

Dr. Alice Toland said, "Hear, hear," and Dr. Clegg frowned at her. But he went on to say, "You've also given us an excellent report on the status of the phobia project, and I'd like to offer you our thanks for that. I don't think we have any more questions or comments. Do we? Dr. Clemens? No? Then I move that we adjourn this meeting."

Dr. Forbes said, "I second the motion," and the meeting broke up. Dr. Clegg and Dr. Clemens left straight away, while Dr. Forbes sat back in his chair, took out his pipe and stuffed it with Klompen Kloggen.

"A man and his pipe," teased Dr. Alice Toland, skirting around the back of his chair. "I'll bet you have a dog and plaid slippers at home."

Dr. Forbes lit up. "As a matter of fact, they used to run advertisements in *Playboy* for this stuff," he said, puffing out of the corner of his mouth. "And they definitely gave the impression that it was one of the quickest ways to get a girl to take off her clothes."

"How long you been smoking it?" asked Dr. Ross, as he tidied up his papers.

"Twelve years."

"And how many girls have taken their clothes off for you?"

"That's a professional secret. Don't you know this is the Ethics Committee?"

Dr. Ross grunted with amusement. He dropped a sheaf of graphs and made a grab for them, just as Dr. Alice Toland tried to grab them too. He bent down to pick them up, and she bent down too, and they almost banged heads. He backed off, his hands raised, like a fighter who doesn't want trouble.

"There—you were right," she said, in a quiet voice. "We never were quite in synch, were we?"

He didn't say anything, just slightly inclined his head to indicate that he was asking her a question. *What are you trying to do? Stir things up again?*

She gathered up the graphs. She was a tall girl, strikingly tall, with long arms and legs. She had straight hair, cut pageboy style, except that it had grown out a little. She was too busy at the hospital, too concerned with the mental health program, and she always forgot salon appointments in any case. But she had fine facial bones, and wide intelligent eyes, and Dr. Ross knew all about the way she could move when she was stirred to.

She gave him the graphs, and he nodded a thank you.

"There isn't any reason we can't be friends, is there?" she asked him.

He shrugged. "Of course not. We're friends already, aren't we? Did anybody say we weren't friends?"

She glanced across at Dr. Forbes. He was puffing, and listening. But when Dr. Ross looked over at him too, he picked up his briefcase, lifted his pipe in salute and said, "It's all right. I was just going anyway."

At the door, he said, "Two."

"Two?" frowned Dr. Ross. "Two what?"

"Two girls took their clothes off for me. My wife and my two-year-old daughter."

"Nice going, Dr. Forbes." Alice Toland laughed.

The door swung shut with a squeak. Dr. Ross said, "Well? What's all this about friends?"

"Peter," she said, "you know exactly what I mean. I did everything wrong. I did all the things I tell my patients not to do, under any circumstances, when they find themselves in a similar situation. It was a case of the shrink who couldn't take her own medicine. But I want you to know that it's all over. No more hysterics. No more pestering. It's over."

Dr. Ross looked away, embarrassed. The whole thing had been a mess. The late-night phone calls. The silly letters. The time he'd come home from a late meeting with Dr. Clegg to find her sitting on the stairs outside of his apartment.

"Please," he said. "It doesn't matter."

"But it *does* matter," she insisted. "You said I was smothering you, and I was. I know that now. Peter, I don't even know who that jealous woman was. She certainly wasn't me. Honestly."

"Okay," he said, "that's fine by me. Now I really have to——"

"Listen," she told him, "all I want is a chance to prove that the smothering woman is gone for good. I want a chance as your friend. As your colleague. As an ardent admirer. Please?"

Dr. Ross tucked his leather briefcase under his arm. "Alice," he said, "this conversation is getting ridiculous. I've never stopped being your friend, and I don't have any intention of stopping now."

"Then we've made up?"

He offered her his arm. "Let's just get going. I have a big afternoon."

"Something to do with the phobia project?"

They stepped out into the corridor, and started to walk. "My agoraphobia patient's taking her first trip out on her own tomorrow."

"Is she scared?"

He nodded. "She's scared all right. But I think she's ready."

"I'd love to read your full notes sometime," she told him. "I think your whole project's terrific."

"I didn't know you were interested in behavioral conditioning. I thought you were the Adlerian to end all Adlerians."

"I'm interested in motivation."

Dr. Ross paused at the door to the corridor marked

TITUS E. FROBISHER WING. "Well," he said, with a
smile that was more than gentle, "I guess we're all interested in motivation, when it comes down to it."

"Peter—" she said.

"I'll see you later," he told her, and pushed his way
through the double swinging doors.

3

As HE WALKED down the green-tiled, echoing corridor, Dr. Ross gave a cheerful salute to the gloomy portrait of Titus E. Frobisher which hung halfway along it. The poor old boy would probably have been horrified if he could have seen the present inmates of the wing he had so proudly presented to the Lakeshore Hospital in 1921. In those days, the sprawling, red-brick infirmary overlooking Lake Erie in the Bratenahl district of Cleveland had been reserved for veterans of the Great War. "A heroes' hospital," Titus E. Frobisher had called it, and in support of those heroes he had foregone the profits from four months' flour milling to build ten private rooms, an operating theater and a small lecture hall.

After World War II, however, under the direction of the legendary Professor Isotow, Lakeshore Hospital had gradually developed a reputation for dealing with shellshock, combat phobia, hyperaggression and all the other grisly injuries that a man's personality can suffer in active military service. By 1955, Lakeshore had transferred the last of its legless airmen and fingerless gun layers to Forest City and Cleveland Metro, and had concentrated on building itself up as one of the country's foremost research centers into disorders of the mind.

At Cleveland Metro the interns referred to Lakeshore as the "Headcase Hilton." But for Peter Ross, Lakeshore had always been his idea of nirvana. The grimness of the building didn't matter. Nor did the fact that it was sited in Cleveland. The most important thing was that Lakeshore could offer him first-rate facilities and the freedom to use them to their ultimate limits. Only here could he take his research patients through the devastating treatment that was needed to prove his most preciously-held theory. Only here could he perfect the therapy which one day the medical world would recognize as "The Ross Solution."

He needed to make his mark on his profession as much as he needed to eat, sleep, exercise, win at ice hockey and make love. More, in fact, because he was one of life's professional succeeders. You only had to look at him, and you could tell. He walked along the corridor of the Titus E. Frobisher wing as if he was bouncing an invisible basketball off the walls, the ceiling and the floor, and catching it every time.

Peter Ross had graduated from the University of California at Santa Cruz as the star of his behavioral psychology class. His father had been dead by then, of an embolism, but his mother had clapped for him, and even wept some tears for him, and afterward, almost shyly, presented him with a Cartier wristwatch. At the age of twenty-seven he had published a landmark paper in *World Mental Health* on irrational responses to external stimuli. At the age of thirty *Time* magazine had mentioned him as "one of the new breed of up-and-at-'em psychotherapists," and published a tiny picture of him, grinning.

And when the Townsend Cereal Foundation had awarded him 2.3 million dollars to perfect a treatment for phobias which had led their sufferers to commit serious crimes, they had noted in their report, "Dr. Peter Frederick Ross, in our opinion, is a determined achiever, and is more strongly motivated to succeed in his research than any other medical beneficiary we have yet come across."

He checked his wristwatch. Digital, because the Cartier was in for cleaning. He wondered if Philippa in the reception office could be persuaded to run out and find him a Reuben sandwich. He reached the green steel door marked *Private,* took out his keys and unlocked it.

Bubba was already waiting for him in the corridor. Bubba was tenser than most of his patients, still wound up about his treatment sessions. He was a West Indian, nearly six-foot three and built like a street fighter. A scar from a broken bottle twisted its way around his chin to the left side of his mouth, and his nose had been broken. But there was a gentleness about him, a strange and almost innocent dignity, which Peter Ross had interpreted from the beginning of Bubba's treatment as a hopeful sign for rehabilitation.

It was only when therapy time came close that Bubba's cool began to crack. He began to bop around, and talk too much, and sweat. You could see him thinking, *Let's get in there and get it over. For Christ's sake let's get it over.*

"How you doing, Dr. Ross?" asked Bubba, as Peter locked the steel door behind him. There was no chance that any of the phobia patients were going to try to make a break for it. They were all too damned sick. But Captain Barnes had laid down that a locked door had to be kept between Dr. Ross's inmates and the outside world at all times. Captain Barnes was not a lover of psychologists, or of social workers, and if the city hadn't leaned on the police department so hard, he would have kept every one of Dr. Ross's patients where he felt they belonged, in the state penitentiary. Captain Barnes had seen the victims of the crimes that Dr. Ross's patients had committed.

"I'm fine, Bubba. The Ethics Committee seems to think we're still ethical, and so we're okay to go ahead."

"Good news, Dr. Ross. Good news."

Dr. Ross continued to walk along the corridor to his office. As he walked, he glanced in at the doors of the old private rooms, where wounded boys from Columbus and Sandusky and Steubenville had once lain with shattered bodies and empty minds, surrounded by flowers. Now these rooms had been converted into bed-sitters, one for each of Dr. Ross's patients. The men were segregated from the women by yet another lockable steel door. "I may not be able to stop them being pampered," Captain Barnes had snapped, "but at least I have the authority to prevent them from procreating."

"Hey, Bubba!" called a voice from one of the rooms, as they passed. Bubba stopped and took a step back. The room was untidy, cluttered with magazines and comics and discarded sneakers, and every wall was thicketed with pictures of John Travolta, Harley-Davidson motorcycles, the Fonz and pink center-spreads from *Hustler*. On the end of the unmade bed sat a thin young greasy-haired boy, not more than eighteen, in a T-shirt marked GENIASES CAN'T SPELL, and jeans.

"Did you finish that twelvepack?" asked the boy. "I can never settle down to watching football without a beer."

"You mean it's a psychological necessity?" called Dr. Ross, who had paused a few yards along the corridor to wait for Bubba.

"Oh, not at all, sir," said the boy. "It's just a physical thirst."

Bubba tried to laugh, but he was too tense to make

it sound very convincing. "I'll catch you later, Johnny," he said. "I'm just going in for the—" He didn't speak the words, or couldn't, and he made a wiggling gesture in the air instead.

Johnny said, "Good luck," and sounded like he meant it. Johnny knew just what Bubba was in for.

Dr. Ross said, "Let's go, Bubba," and they continued their walk. Although Captain Barnes would have objected, the door between the mens' rooms and the women's rooms was usually kept open during the day. Dr. Ross had no fears whatsoever about his patients "procreating." They were all so fiercely wrapped up in the private struggles that were going on inside their heads that even the day-to-day courtesies of "hello" and "how are you?" were a major strain on their sociability.

They were fighting to get back to reality, these people. To rid themselves of unreasonable and irrational fears that could turn them into frenzied, shaking childred—or, worse, into uncontrollable killers. For each one of them, there had been a moment when they had been ready to murder, rather than face their fear.

Barbara was standing by the door of her room as Dr. Ross and Bubba came past. A slim, dark-haired, sensitive-looking woman. Not the kind of woman you would have immediately labeled as a headcase. But a woman whose hurt, questioning eyes never changed expression, and whose fingers were constantly rubbing together as if she was trying to get a smudge off them.

She gave a quick, uncertain smile. Dr. Ross said, "How are you feeling? Do you think you're going to be able to make it tomorrow?"

She nodded. "I'm sure I am. You've told me I'm ready; and if you say I'm ready, then I must be."

"It's your head that has to tell you when you're

ready," said Dr. Ross. "I'm only capable of giving an outside opinion."

She smiled a little. "My head trusts you."

Dr. Ross took her hand between his. He was conscious of Bubba shuffling and bobbing around behind him, and muttering "ba-rub-ah, ba-doo-bah," under his breath, the riff of some unheard panicky tune.

"You're going to be great," Dr. Ross told Barbara, with that infectious grin of his. "You're going to be the first patient to walk out of here cured. And you know what that means, don't you? The earliest parole opportunity possible."

"I'm going to repay you one day," said Barbara softly. "I don't know how, but I will. When I volunteered for this program, I didn't know they were going to put me in the hands of anyone so caring, and so protective, and so goddamned beautiful. But they did, and it was you."

Dr. Ross squeezed her hand, and then turned to Bubba. "Come on, Bubba, let's go get it over. You're starting to make *me* nervous now."

They passed the door of the one-time operating theater, which Dr. Ross now used as an office. There was a wide desk, a revolving leather chair and a row of shelves packed with bound volumes of the *Journal of General Psychology,* the *Journal of Personality* and *Perceptual and Motor Skills.*

"Come in for a moment," said Dr. Ross. "I want to get your records before I begin. Sit down. Relax, if you can."

"I'll stand, thanks," said Bubba. "Ain't no way I can keep myself still when I'm thinking about those—"

Dr. Ross raised his hand. "Don't start talking yourself into a fear situation before you've even started. You can lick it. You know that as well as I do."

Bubba shrugged, and shuffled around the room while

Dr. Ross collected his papers. On the desk were three framed photographs. One of a strikingly pretty girl, blond, and very wide-eyed. It was signed "To Peter —with all the love that ever was, Jenny." Another of a family group, probably taken in the early '50s, a father and a mother and two small children, all screwing up their eyes against the sun. The third of a serious-looking man, very similar in appearance to Peter Ross himself, except that his hair was shorter and straighter, and there was a hardness in his eyes which Peter Ross never had.

"This your pa?" asked Bubba, picking the photograph up.

Dr. Ross glanced across at him, and for a moment looked as if he was about to snap, *Put that down*. But he nodded and said "That's right," and went on sorting out Bubba's papers.

"Never knew my pa," said Bubba, joggling around the room again. "Only saw my ma once too. Fat, she was. Fatter'n me. I reckon my ma could've been useful extra help in a street fight. Whip, whup, with the old radio antenna, no trouble. You ever see anybody whipped with the old radio antenna, Dr. Ross?"

Dr. Ross shook his head.

"Whoo, that's something," said Bubba. "That can lay the whole cheek right open, right through to your teeth. I seen that, and quite a few of them kids tried it on me, too. But that didn't frighten me none. Only thing ever gets me going is those—"

"Bubba, for Christ's sake!" shouted Dr. Ross. "You're making it worse for yourself! Now, will you calm down, and get your mind clear, and start thinking positive thoughts."

Bubba took a deep breath. "Okay," he said, with his eyes closed. "I'm thinking 'em. Positive, positive thoughts."

"Right, then," said Dr. Ross. He paused for a moment to pick up a pair of ice-hockey boots to check the blades. Then he said, "Let's go, huh?"

They walked through to the room which had once been Titus E. Frobisher's lecture hall. Now, the students' benches had all been taken out, and it looked more like a television studio, with a generator, projectors and dozens of black snaking cables. Bubba trod over the cables with nervous caution, until he reached The Box.

The Box was the essence of the Ross treatment. It was The Box which had taken up nearly half-a-million dollars of the therapy program's total budget. In the dimness of the old lecture hall, crisscrossed by narrow-beamed spotlights, it looked like some kind of strange extraterrestrial construction which had just arrived from the Hyades.

On the outside The Box appeared to be complicated and makeshift. But once the patient opened the door in its side and stepped in, he found himself in a totally blank, white room. The door closed, and he was sealed off from sound, from color, from any human contact. Inside of this Box, he was going to meet his most terrible fears face to face, and on his own.

Dr. Ross walked over to the operating console and flicked a few switches. Red, green and amber lights appeared on the console in front of him. He pressed two buttons, and there was a whirring sound as the movie projectors automatically selected the sequences he wanted, and rewound them.

Bubba was waiting by the open door of The Box, his forehead glistening with sweat. His face was as ghastly as that of a man who has just been ordered to step into his own coffin.

"Dr. Ross," he said, and there was a hint of pleading in his voice.

Dr. Ross looked up from the console. "Yes? What is it, Bubba?"

"You know what you said to Barbara? About her head being ready?"

"What about it?"

"Well, Dr. Ross, I'm not sure my head's quite ready for this treatment session yet. I mean, if I could maybe go back a couple of sessions, just look at the pictures in the book like we did before—"

"Bubba—"

....The West Indian was walking back across the hall now, skirting around the cables, and his hands were spread out in a desperate appeal. The front of his gray regulation shirt was dark with sweat.

"I know what you're going to tell me, Dr. Ross. I know. But I'm not sure I can really take it in there. I mean, I know how good that Box is. That Box is amazing. I've seen what it's done for Barbara, you know, and Henry—but, Dr. Ross, I really don't want to go in there."

Dr. Ross sat down on his swiveling console seat. He looked up at Bubba for a while, with his hand over his mouth, and then he looked away, at some distant event or object that Bubba couldn't perceive.

"Bubba," he said quietly. His therapy-session voice, modulated and persuasive. "Are you going to let yourself down? Now? After all you've been through already?"

"Dr. Ross, I know that I can make up the time, but—"

"You *can't* make up the time, Bubba. You're my slowest patient already. This therapy program has been awarded a lavish budget to continue its work, but even lavishness is limited. The time is rapidly drawing near when I've got to show results. Results means cured patients. Results means you facing up to what goes on in The Box, and coming out of there as cool as you went in."

"But I'm not cool now, Dr. Ross. No way am I cool."

"I know. For Christ's sake, I know. I had the same kind of fear myself. But I overcame it. I faced up to it and I saw it for what it was. Irrational, unreasonable and absurd."

"Dr. Ross—"

Dr. Ross shook his head. "I'm not going to listen to you any more, Bubba. You're going to get into The Box, and we're going to go through the treatment."

Bubba stood straight, his face as glossy as a black patent-leather shoe. "And supposing I won't?"

"Then I pick up this phone and call Captain Barnes, and you'll be back in the penitentiary before you can draw breath. Two life sentences, isn't it? Just because that poor old woman tried to save herself and give you those necklaces."

"I thought they were—" said Bubba abruptly, and then stopped himself, wiping the sweat from his face with the back of his hand.

"Okay," said Dr. Ross. "So, into The Box, Bubba. You know what you've got to gain, and you know what you've got to lose."

Bubba stood there for a long time, breathing in and out, the way a weightlifter does before he attempts a record lift. Then he nodded, and turned, and walked straight back to The Box, stepping inside and closing the door behind him. This time, he made an effort to walk straight over the cables, although he wouldn't actually tread on any of them.

Dr. Ross waited for a minute, and then he leaned forward to a microphone on the console, tapped it to make sure it was live and said, "Are you ready, Bubba?"

Silence. And then, *"Okay."*

Dr. Ross, his face impassive in the dim glow from

the telltale lights on the console, flicked switches. The projectors began to whirr, and he sat back in his chair, motionless but attentive. After a while, he reached out and flicked one more switch, and an image of Bubba appeared on a closed-circuit television screen on his right-hand side.

Bubba's eyes were closed. Tight. His while face was clenched in an expression of total rejection and total fear.

"Open your eyes, Bubba," Dr. Ross directed him gently.

Bubba shook his head.

"Come on, Bubba, open your eyes."

"I can't."

"You must. If you can't open your eyes, you'll have failed. You'll have failed yourself and you'll have failed me."

"Dr. Ross, I—"

"Open your eyes, damn you! Open your eyes and see what's out there! It's your fear, and you've got to face it!"

Shaking, as if he was suffering from chronic pneumonia, Bubba slowly opened his eyes. He stared at the walls around him and his jaw stiffened in utter horror. There was no question of him closing his eyes now. He was too frightened.

On the walls, all around him, were dozens of snakes. Sliding and writhing and twisting over each other, rattlesnakes and water moccasins and sidewinders, dry and slithery and flickering their tongues.

"Oh, Jesus," he was mumbling. "Oh, Jesus, let this be over."

But the snakes only seemed to slide nearer, and for the first time he heard their rattling and hissing. He was locked tight with fear. Unable to move. Unable to turn around, because he knew the snakes were behind him, too.

(And for a split second he remembered the small gray-haired woman who had picked up the tray from her dressing table and flung it at him, and all those sliding shining things had poured out at his feet, and all he had thought was, *Snakes, for God's sake, snakes,* and struck out at her in such terror and with such ferocity that it had taken a surgical saw to remove the knife blade from her breastbone.)

Bubba's face went gray. He could feel his knees shaking and he wasn't sure how much longer he could stand. A rattlesnake close to his right side began to rear up and perform a curious sideways slither that soaked his fear with the coldness of complete dread.

I told him I couldn't take it. I told him I couldn't take it. These snakes are just too damned much. How can I ever get used to snakes. Oh, Jesus don't let them come any closer. I know they're not real. I know they're only movies. But, oh, Jesus, don't let them come any closer.

After ten minutes Dr. Ross reached forward again and flicked the switch marked BACK PROJECTION OFF. Then he sat back and waited for Bubba to come out. He always let them come out in their own time. It helped them adjust to the fact that it was actually all over, and they were still in one piece.

The door in the side of The Box swung open, and Bubba came out. He walked as if he were drunk.

Dr. Ross said, "How do you feel? Are you okay?"

Bubba nodded, his eyes swiveling in aimless shock. "I'm okay," he said hoarsely. "I just need to lie down."

"Was it better this time?"

Bubba nodded again.

"They didn't scare you so much?"

"No."

"You think you can stay inside for longer tomorrow?"

"I don't know."

"Do you want to try?"

"I just don't know, Dr. Ross."

"Your pulse rate is still way up when the snakes first appear on the screen. So's your respiration."

"I can't help it, Dr. Ross. It's just the way I am."

"But you're not so scared?"

"I don't think so."

"You don't *think* so? You just said you weren't for sure."

"Well, I—well, I'm not so scared as I was. I'm better."

Dr. Ross put his arm around Bubba and led him to the door. "Bubba," he said, "it's working. Your responses are improving all the time. Slowly, I know— but that's because you're expecting too much. What you're going to have to do next time is relax. Really relax."

"Okay, Dr. Ross. Can I go now?"

"Sure. I'll come around later and make up the report. You just have a rest, and think about what happened today. Okay?"

Bubba hesitated at the door. "Dr. Ross," he said.

"What is it, Bubba?"

"I hope I'm not letting you down, Dr. Ross."

Dr. Ross grinned. "I want to tell you something, Bubba. I've gotten this therapy program together in the teeth of the most aggressive establishment opposition you've ever seen in your life. The police don't like it, the prison service doesn't like it, and eighty percent of the top psychotherapists in the whole damned U.S.A. don't like it. If it hadn't been for City Hall wanting to show that they were doing something meaningful to solve the crime problem in Cleveland, we probably wouldn't have had this program at all. So just remember one thing. There's a whole lot of people in this city who want to see you back in prison. There are probably just as many who want to see you dead, all of you. So if you fail to respond to this therapy—which you won't, I promise you—there's only one person you're going to be letting down. That person is you."

Bubba looked down at the floor. "You know something," he said. "You're a good man, Dr. Ross. I don't think we honestly deserve you."

Dr. Ross slapped him on the back. "Whether you deserve me or not, Bubba, you got me. So make the most of me while you can."

4

DR. ROSS SPENT the rest of the afternoon working on his patients' files. There were pages of results to be marked up, progress curves to be drawn, reports to be written. There was nothing simple or easy about taking five convicted killers through a totally experimental therapy program, especially against the determined opposition of the police department and the prison administration.

Except for having Dr. Clegg in goal for him, it was like playing ice hockey against a team that outnumbered him one hundred to one. What's more, it was crucial to his entire career that he win.

There were five of them, three men and two women. All of them volunteers, each of them hand-picked by Dr. Ross himself from seventy-eight disturbed murderers. Five different killers with five different phobias, from Bubba's fear of snakes to Barbara's fear of open spaces.

Dr. Ross filled in the latest information in Bubba's file in neat, orderly writing. Bernard (Bubba) King, thirty-five years old, convicted for armed robbery and manslaughter. An orphan, brought up in a home on Haig Avenue in Columbus, within hailing distance of the Ohio State Hospital for the Insane. There was no

historical reason for his phobia that Bubba could remember, although he could vividly recall an orphanage
visit to see *The Living Desert,* during which he had
been carried screaming and hysterical to the lobby.

Then there was Johnny Venuti, twenty, born in Toledo of a seventeen-year-old prostitute, who used to
shut him for hours in a closet while she turned tricks
to make a living. Johnny was a severe claustrophobe,
unable to stay in a room with the door closed. He had
struck a guard with a chair at a juvenile detention home
when the guard had attempted to lock him in; and the
guard had later died.

Henry Lawson, fifty-six, also known as Henry Charles
and Henry Pierce, was a small-time confidence trickster
and petty housebreaker from Shabbona Park, Chicago,
also born, ironically, within a few blocks of a sani-
tarium for the mentally disturbed, the Chicago-Read.
He was a habitual criminal with a police record as thick
as a telephone directory, but he had only turned killer
when a cop had cornered him during the course of a
minor robbery. Henry had been faced with the choice
of jumping from a second-story window, or shooting at
the policeman who was just about to catch him. Henry's
fear of heights had led him to pull the trigger.

Laura Adams, twenty-three, came from Barberton,
near Akron. She had been an assistant in a drugstore
on Exchange Street, Akron, until the night of April
10th, seven years ago. Then, walking home from the
store, she had been followed by seven students from the
University of Akron, all young and drunk and full of
themselves. They had chased her, frightened her and
eventually raped her in a parking lot, on a heap of old
tires. Five years later, still terrified by men, Laura had
stuck the points of a pair of kitchen scissors into the
eyes of a horny but genial drunk who had accosted her
in her apartment in Cleveland.

Barbara Grey, twenty-seven, was an agoraphobe. She had been born in Queens, New York, and brought up until the age of twenty as a well-balanced, well-educated city girl. At the age of twenty-one, however, she had married an intense would-be screenwriter, who had taken her out to Kaycee, Wyoming, population 272, to "find creative solitude." Two months later, the would-be screenwriter had left her, and she had been abandoned with a small child and more open space than a Queens girl could handle. A well-meaning friend had invited her to Cleveland to stay for a while, and one morning had tried to persuade her to go out for a walk. Barbara, in front of witnesses, had pushed her friend from a third-floor apartment down the stairwell. All because she couldn't face the great outside.

Five people who could have led normal, useful lives. Five people who could have been happy. You could have passed any one of them in the street and not even noticed them. Yet each of them was in the grip of a private fear so overwhelming that they would rather spend the rest of their lives in custody than face up to it.

Dr. Ross closed the files, stretched back in his chair and rubbed his eyes. From his gold-beaded frame on the far side of the desk, his dead father watched him with the same stern uncompromising expression as always. *When I say you have to swim, son, you have to swim. No two ways about it.*

Dr. Ross whispered, "I'll swim, Dad. You watch me."

The telephone rang, and he reached forward and picked it up. "Ross," he said abruptly.

"Peter?" asked a soft voice.

"Oh, Jenny. Hi. How are you doing?"

"I've been lecturing today. How are you?"

"Tired. I did a session with Bubba this afternoon, and I've just been through the case histories."

"How did the Ethics Committee go?"

"Okay. I got through. But Sara Clemens was kind of aggressive. She said my patients came out of their treatment looking battered."

"Well, don't they?"

"Sure they do. It's what the whole treatment's all about."

There was a pause, and then Jenny said, "Are you free tonight?"

"Free? I'm never free. My apartment belongs to the Cleveland Savings Bank, my days belong to Townsend Cereals, my intellect belongs to my patients and my heart belongs to you."

"Do you think the bank and the cereals and the patients will release you long enough to come around to my place for supper?"

"Jenny, I can't. I have Barbara going out tomorrow morning. I have the hockey game tomorrow afternoon. If I don't clear all my paperwork this evening, I'm going to be snowed under."

"What are you going to eat?"

"Wendy's finest, I expect."

"Peter, you can't live like that."

"Jenny, I have to. I have a limited time to complete this work and that's it. You don't think that the Ohio State Prison Board cares about my digestion, do you?"

"No," she said gently, "but *I* do."

"That's because you love me madly."

She was quiet for a moment, and then she said, "You guessed."

"Listen," he said, "you're coming to the game, aren't you?"

"Of course."

"Well, I'll see you then. And just remember that I may even love you madly, too."

She said, simply, "Enjoy your hamburger," and hung

up. Dr. Ross held the dead receiver in his hand for a while, grinning, and then hung up too. It was good to know that there was somebody out there in the early-evening city of Cleveland, amid all those sparkling lights and crowded streets, somebody who really cared.

He left the hospital shortly after ten o'clock. The security guard had come on duty at nine, and had already locked the intervening door between the men's and the women's sections, and was sitting by the outside door reading a dog-eared paperback novel. It was the first time Dr. Ross had seen him in spectacles.

"Good night, Jack," he said. "What's the book?"

The guard took off his glasses and looked embarrassed. "It's nothing. Some story about the president, getting possessed by the devil. *The Hell Candidate*."

Dr. Ross patted him on the back and grinned. "If it tells you how to perform an exorcism, let me know," he said. "I've got quite a few devils to chase out myself."

His Porsche 911 was the last car in the parking lot. The night was foggy now, and the street lamp wore soft haloes of light, like dandelion puffballs. *Taraxacum officinale,* he thought, the common wayside dandelion. He thought it was funny the way things stuck in your mind after all these years. He climbed into the car, slammed the door and switched on the engine.

It wasn't far to his apartment. A few hundred yards northeast on Lake Shore Boulevard, and then south on 105th Street. He lived in one of those staid, reddish brick houses overlooking the Shakespeare Garden, close to the Cleveland Art Museum. They had seen better days, these houses, and far more select residents, but they were still ample and comfortable, and the rooms were airy and large.

He let himself in to his apartment on the third floor. He switched on the lamps in the living room one by one, and then turned on the stereo. It was soft, nighttime music, the sort he usually called "Milwaukee Piano Bar." But after a tough day with his five patients, and a difficult time with the Ethics Committee, it was just what he felt like. He went to the glass and chrome drinks table and poured himself a Glenfiddich, straight up, no ice.

There was no doubt this was a man's apartment. It was decorated in dark brown leathers, creams and shiny metals. A large abstract of two cream and white rhomboids hung above the brown sofa; and the glass tables were carefully arranged with magazines. *Fortune, Playboy* and *Psychology Today*.

In the kitchenette, with its Neff stove and all its gadgets, there was a grainy black and white blow-up of Peter Ross himself, playing ice hockey. It had been taken three years ago, in Toronto, in the days when he had discovered that he had a natural abrasive flair for ice hockey, and that he was passionately interested in the study of phobias. A tall slow-speaking Canuck called Dubuque had coached him on the ice; but when he had sought help on phobias from Dr. Guillaume Laurier at the University of Toronto, he had received nothing but discouragement.

"Irrational fears can only be minimized by therapy," Dr. Laurier had insisted. "You can educate phobia patients to adopt a prearranged pattern of behavior which will help them to survive in a crisis. For instance, you can condition a claustrophobia patient to concentrate on something else altogether until he is able to escape from his claustrophobic situation. But you cannot eradicate phobias altogether—and especially not by violent confrontation. That is like trying to teach a child to overcome its fear of the water by throwing it straight into the pool—using the Implosion Therapy principle."

Dr. Ross had grinned at that, and nodded. Implosion therapy had worked for him—why couldn't it work for other people? Maybe it was time that Dr. Laurier and the rest of the psychotherapeutic establishment had their ideas of what could and couldn't be treated turned upside down.

He kicked off his Gucci loafers, rolled up his shirt sleeves and sat down in his armchair. Tomorrow was going to be the first field test for the Ross theory, and it was going to be his first practical success. If Barbara could walk the streets of Cleveland without feeling that the sky was going to fall in on her, then he would know for certain that he was on the right track, and only a few weeks away from completing his work. After Barbara, he'd test Johnny, and after Johnny, Laura. This was the moment when his five children were all going to be thrown into the pool.

Over in the corner of the room, by the window, stood a gray steel filing cabinet. This was where he kept all the duplicate records of his therapy's progress. There was a drawer for each one of his patients, with Barbara Grey's name on the top drawer.

He stood up and walked across to the cabinet with his drink in his hand. Maybe he ought to go over her papers one more time, just to make sure there were no flaws in her treatment which he hadn't noticed before. No unexpected angles. No quirks. But, after a moment, he turned away from the cabinet and walked back across the apartment. He knew that Barbara was as ready as she was ever going to be. He'd been over her records time and time again, until he practically knew every palpitation and pulse rate by heart. Taking her file out and going over it was going to be more hassle than it was worth.

He decided to go out and get himself a hamburger, and then come back and apply himself to Henry's vital-response graph. He could see his own face in the blow-up photograph in the kitchen, gritty and determined.

The day that Dubuque had taken that, he had been winning. It was a winner's face.

He tugged on a cableknit pullover which he had left on the side of the sofa, took a five-dollar bill out of his wallet, found his keys and opened his apartment door. He turned off the main light before he went, although he left the table lamps on.

That left the gray filing cabinet shadowed by the wall, so that it was almost impossible for a casual visitor to make out the thin wire which stretched from the handle of Barbara Grey's drawer, around the side of the cabinet and into a shining brass detonator. The detonator itself was buried in a large flattish lump of doughy-looking stuff which an expert would have immediately recognized as plastic explosive.

In U.S. Army training manuals, the same amount of explosive was recommended for such tasks as blowing open heavy steel doors, or destroying a light tank.

5

HE CAME TO the door. Barbara was sitting on the edge of her bed, dressed in a smart but outdated coat of white flecked wool, and a striped blouse. He had given her a sedative last night, but she still looked as if she hadn't slept. Her fingers were rubbing anxiously against each other, and she obviously found it difficult to smile.

Laura was standing in the corner of Barbara's room, her dark hair tousled, smoking a cigarette. She was wearing a white blouse with a Peter Pan collar, buttoned up to the neck, and baggy jeans. It was strangely noticeable that she wore no jewelry at all, and no make-up, although she was pert and pretty enough to look good as she was.

Dr. Ross said to Barbara, "You ready?"

Barbara gave him a tight smile and nodded.

Laura said loudly, "I sure wish it was my turn."

"Your turn'll come," said Barbara, as if she was anxious to avoid a lengthy discussion.

Laura crushed out her cigarette in an ashtray marked PROPERTY OF LAKESHORE HOSPITAL. "The way I'm going, I'll be dead last," she said.

Dr. Ross gave her a quick but cautioning glance. It meant cool it, keep it down. This is Barbara's big day, and the last thing she needs is to hear about anybody else's problems. Whenever any one of his patients reached a crucial stage in her therapy, Dr. Ross always encouraged the others to treat her like a star.

Everybody needs applause at one time or another, he thought. Applause is what makes it all worthwhile.

Barbara stood up and collected her pocketbook. "Well," she said with a nervous flick of her hair, "I guess we'd better go."

Laura said, "Good luck, honey. Say hello to that big wide yonder for me."

Dr. Ross took Barbara's arm. "Come on. Everything's going to be fine."

Together, they left the women's section and walked along the corridor. Johnny was standing at the door of his room, and he gave her a little finger-wave as she passed, but neither of them said a word. Johnny knew exactly what terrors were racing around inside of Barbara's mind, and just how little she wanted to talk to anybody else.

Barbara, he knew, was thinking about The Box. About those comfortable, back-projected walls which gradually began to open out, wider and wider, until they revealed stunning open spaces. Skies, deserts, wide city streets—vast and uncompromising distances that stretched beyond the eyesight, beyond the imagination, beyond the point of human coherence.

Johnny knew that Barbara had huddled in that Box, hugging herself in terror, the same way that he had. Eyes closed, mind closed, with nothing but the coaxing voice of Dr. Ross to see her through.

"Open your eyes, Barbara," he would have said. "Open your eyes and take a look at those open spaces."

And she would have opened her eyes and felt as if gravity had evaporated, and that she was dropping upward into the sky.

They reached the swinging doors that led out into the

hospital's main reception area. The plastic-tiled floor
was as glossy as the surface of a lake. Then they were
approaching the revolving door that led out of the hospital itself to the front parking lot, and Dr. Ross, holding Barbara's arm, was acutely conscious of the way her
feet were slowing themselves down, and of the way the
muscles in her cheeks were flexing.

They passed the reception area. A nurse smiled at
them fixedly from behind her hedge of plastic flowers.
A disembodied voice on the intercom said, *"Dr. Forbes
to Neurotherapy, please. Dr. Forbes."*

"Here we go," said Dr. Ross, and Barbara clenched
her teeth as they pushed their way through the doors
and out into the blinding reality of a gray midmorning
in Cleveland.

Barbara stumbled on the top step outside, and Dr.
Ross had to steady her. Her face was stiff, and she was
breathing in tight, shallow gasps. She didn't look at the
sky, or the windblown evergreens around the parking
lot, but concentrated instead on staring at Dr. Ross.

"Tell me I'm doing fine," she whispered.

He grinned at her. "You're doing fine. My car's just
along here."

He led her along to his Porsche. She stood beside
him, chewing at her lips, while he found his keys and
unlocked it. "It's a nice car," she said unsteadily. "I
really go for cars like this. They're small, you know.
Cozy."

"What do you need with cozy cars?" smiled Dr. Ross.
"You're a woman of the world now. This is all yours,
for you to enjoy."

He stretched his arm out expansively. She smiled and
nodded, but she wouldn't look where he was pointing.
She didn't want to see those faraway trees, or that gray
and empty sky. She didn't want to see the endless
expanse of that parking lot. Not just yet.

She climbed into the car and sat cradling her knees. Dr. Ross climbed in beside her, picked out his ignition key and started the engine.

"You're doing fine," he repeated. "It's a great big world out there, and you have to take it little by little."

He released the handbrake, backed up and turned out of the lot. What he didn't notice, as he shifted the Porsche into first, and then quickly into second, was Dr. Alice Toland, standing by her car only a few yards away. Dr. Toland had just finished a morning's analysis with a Cleveland supermarket owner who had been stealing his own goods, and she was about to drive home. She brushed the hair away from her face as she watched Dr. Ross leave the hospital entrance with Barbara, and she frowned.

Dr. Toland hesitated for a moment. Then, on an impulse, she climbed into her Zephyr, started it up and swung out of her parking space with a squeal of tires. She reached the hospital gates, looked around and caught sight of Dr. Ross's Porsche just as it disappeared behind a refrigerated truck. She turned left on Lake Shore Boulevard and followed.

There—he was making a right down 105th. She kept after him, her fingers drumming on the wheel.

Supposing he saw her? she thought. Well, there was no harm in that. She had been going home anyway, and if she wanted to take a detour past the park, what law said she couldn't?

She switched on the car radio. It was playing *Better Love Next Time, Baby*. These damn songs. Irritated, she turned it off.

Dr. Ross, driving his Porsche, was silent. He was watching the traffic and he was watching Barbara. He didn't see the lipstick-red Zephyr in his rear-view mirror, although he would have recognized it immediately if he had. It had been awkwardly parked outside of his apartment that night he had come home and found Alice sitting on his stairs, blotchy-eyed and more than half-drunk.

Barbara said, "I'm scared out of my mind. I hope you understand that."

"You're not scared," Dr. Ross told her. "You're just worried that those feelings are going to come back. Well, I can tell you one thing for sure. They're not."

"Where are we going?" she asked him.

"To a little park, not far away from here."

"Oh?" She sounded dampened. "What happens then?"

He pulled out to overtake a parked truck. "Then you'll do what you've been working and suffering for all these weeks in The Box. You'll meet your phobia head on, and realize you've beaten it."

"You really think I can?"

He grinned. "I'm sure of it. You're my ace volunteer."

Barbara licked her lips. "So I get out in this park, and I walk. . . ."

"That's right. You walk a few blocks among the trees and the flowers, and then you leave the park and start heading downtown. That's all you have to do."

She looked at him for a long time. She didn't look at the trees and the shadows passing the car window.

"What if I panic?" she said, with a catch in her voice.

"You won't."

"But what if I do?"

He was driving under Route 6 now, toward Shakespeare Gardens and his own apartment. "You're pretty well cured," he insisted. "You won't panic, and that's it. All you have to do, when you've finished your walk, is make your way back to the hospital. You've got ten dollars for a taxi. Or, if you feel you can't manage that, come to my apartment. I'll be working there all through lunch."

"I don't know where your apartment is," she said tensely.

"I'll show you. It isn't far. Sometimes I jog to the hospital instead of driving."

She said, "The police won't—"

He waved his hand reassuringly. "The police won't give you any trouble at all. All your papers have been cleared at headquarters for letting you out, and Captain Barnes has seen all of your reports. Now, look, here's my apartment here."

He drew into the curb, and pointed up to his front window. "That's it. Number Eleven Argyle Street. Third floor. You got it?"

She nodded. "Eleven Argyle. Okay. I can remember that."

Dr. Ross glanced in his mirror and pulled out from the curb. He still didn't catch sight of the red Zephyr, because it had stopped on the other side of the road, next to the park. He turned the Porsch around, and drove toward the main entrance to the park, further down. Then he climbed out and walked around the car to open Barbara's door.

She sat tight in her seat, all bunched up. She didn't budge.

"Come on," he said, in his soft, encouraging voice. "You can make it."

She looked up at him, and if it wasn't fear in her eyes, it was something very close.

"Come on," he coaxed her again. "You can get right out there and lick that phobia face-to-face."

Barbara swallowed hard. Then, shakily, she stepped out of the car.

"That's the park entrance," said Dr. Ross. "Walk straight through there and keep going. When you get to the other side, keep on walking that way and it'll take you downtown."

"It won't matter if I only take a short walk, will it?" she asked in a whisper.

"As long or as short as you want. I'll be working in my apartment for at least a couple of hours."

She took his hand, clutched it. "I really have beaten it, haven't I?" she implored him. Her teeth were chattering as if she was cold.

Dr. Ross kissed her, once, on the forehead.

"You've beaten it," he said.

He stood and watched her as she walked slowly across the sidewalk to the park entrance. She turned when she was there, and stared back at him. He waved, and she waved in return. Then, as if she had made up her mind to get hold of her terrors by the throat, she went quickly off through the crowds of lunchtime strollers and disappeared.

Dr. Ross stood there on his own for a time without moving. Then he let his chin drop on to his chest. It wasn't until three or four minutes had gone by that he went back to his car and drove it around to the front of his apartment.

Sitting in the driver's seat of her parked Zephyr, Dr. Alice Toland lit a cigarette and watched him as he locked his car, bounded athletically up the front steps and let himself into his house. Peter the athlete, she thought to herself. Athlete's mind, athlete's body. How can the rest of us poor mortals possibly keep up?

6

MRS. CASEY WAS cleaning his apartment when he opened the door. She was spraying wax everywhere as if it was Christmas, and singing *I Got the Music in Me* at the top of her warbling voice.

"Dr. Ross," she said. "Now there's a surprise."

"Hello, Mrs. Casey," said Dr. Ross. "How's the angel of hygiene today?"

"Oh, you will tease me," Mrs. Casey smirked, flapping her duster at him in mock coyness. She was a short, plump woman, wrapped up in a floral apron, and she'd been cleaning these apartments for fifteen years. Her husband had been a deckhand on the aircraft carrier *Harper's Ferry* during the Korean War, and had lost both his hands when a Voodoo jet snapped an arrester wire. "Mr. Casey's will to work went with his hands," Mrs. Casey always used to say, but whatever the psychology behind it, Mrs. Casey spent ten hours a day cleaning apartments and helping in a school canteen while Mr. Casey sat in O'Neill's Bar on Buckeye Road and demonstrated his proficiency in picking up glasses of Jamieson's whiskey with metal hands.

Dr. Ross went into the kitchenette, opened the icebox and took out a glass of V-8. He drank it slowly as he walked around the apartment, unbuttoning his cuff with his free hand.

"Isn't it terrible warm for the time of year?" Mrs. Casey said. She had finished polishing the glass coffee table, and now she moved across to the corner where the filing cabinet stood. She gave the top a good spray with her polish, wiped it over and flicked at the front of it with her duster.

"Isn't it though." Dr. Ross grinned. He went to the window and looked out across the street toward the park. Barbara was there somewhere, walking alone amid all of that open space. *Good luck, Barbara,* he thought. *If you can beat that phobia today, then we're winning all the way. I may be calm, and I may be professional, but my heart's beating with yours today, like a father's heart beats with his child's.*

"Is it something special you've come back for?" asked Mrs. Casey.

"Unh?" he asked abstractedly.

"I didn't think I'd be seeing you today at all," she said. "I was only saying to Mr. Casey this morning that it's been months now since I saw you. Although I've never seen Mrs. Armitage in apartment twenty-six at all in six years, if you can believe it. There's a person who keeps herself to herself."

"I've, uh, I've got a whole lot of reports to write up," said Dr. Ross.

"But isn't it the game this afternoon?"

He checked his watch. "Oh, sure. But that's not until two-thirty."

"Sure and it's one-forty already. You'd better be getting your skates on. Oh! Now did you listen to me then? You'd better be getting your skates on, I said, and if that isn't a joke."

"One-forty?" asked Dr. Ross. He pressed his digital watch again. "I've got five minutes of twelve."

Mrs. Casey came across and peered at his watch. "Is it one of your gadgetal watches, now? My nephew had one for his birthday and sure it didn't work at all."

"I'd better get going," said Dr. Ross. "Listen, Mrs. Casey, it's remotely possible that a girl called Barbara Grey may come by. She's a patient of mine from the hospital. If you see her, can you ask her to make her own way back to the hospital—that's if she feels she can manage it. If not, she's welcome to wait here."

He went across to the filing cabinet and put his hand on the drawer marked BARBARA GREY. "Maybe I should take her papers along with me and give them a final check at the rink." Dr. Ross pulled the drawer out a fraction.

"Don't you ever stop that working?" asked Mrs. Casey. "You'll work yourself to death, the way you're going."

"You're right for once, Mrs. Casey," said Dr. Ross, changing his mind and shutting it again. "Today, I'll just go play ice hockey."

He went to his bedroom, opened his cupboard door and took out his kitbag. "You won't forget about Barbara, will you?" he asked, as he shrugged on his jacket. "This is a big day for her. First time she's been out on her own."

"You just go along," said Mrs. Casey. "I've looked after eight of my own."

Dr. Ross ran quickly down the apartment stairs to the street. He threw his kitbag into the back of his Porsche, gunned the engine and roared off toward the ice rink.

Across the street Dr. Alice Toland was sitting on a park bench, reading a copy of the *Plain Dealer*. Her eyes narrowed when she saw Dr. Ross's car pull away into the traffic, and she stood up, folding the newspaper as she watched him go. Then she turned and looked up toward the window of his apartment, where she glimpsed Mrs. Casey giving a final polish to the silver ice-hockey trophies on the windowsill.

7

As soon as she was halfway across the park, Barbara knew that she was in trouble. She had known that the sky was going to be big, and she had known that there wasn't going to be anything around her to keep her feeling secure and cozy, but the reality of outdoors was far noisier and far emptier and far more hostile than she had ever imagined.

Sōmehow, when she had crouched in The Box, there had always been that one tiny crumb of reassurance in the back of her mind that it wasn't real—that the wide-open spaces all around her were only back-projections, and that she was really sitting in a safe, enclosed room. Now, that one crumb of reassurance had been swept away, and Barbara Grey was out on her own with nothing but the world.

She walked quickly, as if she was afraid that she might be plucked off the winding path and hurtled into the gray and endless skies. She passed dozens of people, but she didn't see them. All she could see was the opposite gate, jumbled in her panicky vision like *cinéma vérité,* and all she could think of was reaching the street and calling a taxi.

She collided with a woman pushing a baby in a stroller, but she didn't even stop to apologize. "Why the

hell don't you look where you're walking, lady?" the
woman called after her.

*I daren't. It's all gone wrong. I thought I was going
to be cured but I'm not. I'm just as frightened of sky
and trees and wide-open spaces as I always was. They
seem to stretch and stretch in all directions, leaving me
open and defenseless. It's as bad as Kaycee, Wyoming.
All that vast and curving sky, all that deserted and
lonesome land. I can't make it, even though I want to.*

She tried to think of Dr. Ross as she walked. What
was Dr. Ross going to say when she turned up at his
apartment and told him she hadn't been able to make
it? His star patient, flunking out. Maybe, just for him,
she could manage to make it just a little further. Maybe
as far as a bar, or a restaurant. Then she could wait for
a while, and catch a taxi back to the hospital. He
wouldn't know that she'd cheated. Unless he was having her followed, of course, or unless the police were
keeping an eye on her.

She wanted to turn around to see if Dr. Ross or one
of the hospital assistants was behind her, but she knew
that the distance she had covered across the park was
too wide, and that she didn't dare to look at it. Three
hundred feet of gray asphalt path, endless miles of sky.
She walked more quickly, almost breaking into a run,
and a benchful of Cleveland's senior citizens watched
her go by with unabashed curiosity.

"She sure looks like she's running from something,"
one of them remarked, interrupting his friend's résumé
of last night's celebrity golf game.

The friend looked around. "Sure don't see nothing.
Maybe she's got herself a bus to catch."

Barbara, at last, reached the opposite side of the
park. Her breath came in harsh, restricted gasps, and
she could feel the perspiration under her arms. God,
there was so much open space. So many wide sidewalks.

So many people and cars. She stumbled along for two or three blocks, looking desperately around for a taxi, but none came by. The panic was rising inside her now like vomit, and her mind a mishmash of passing images, like a smashed mirror held together with sticky tape.

Oh God, Dr. Ross, I can't.

A taxi passed her by, and stopped on a red light at the next intersection. Somehow, she managed to sway across to it and claw at the door handle. The cabbie wound down the window and said, "Beat it, lady. I don't take drunks."

"Please," she said, hoarsely. "Please—I'm not drunk."

"Forget it," said the cabbie. "Whether you're drunk or not, I'm not taking you."

"Please, I'm ill. I want you to take me to the hospital."

"What's the matter?" asked the cabbie suspiciously. "You having a baby? I don't know nothing about delivering no babies."

"I'm just sick. I need to get back to Lakeshore."

"Lakeshore? You mean the nuthouse?"

She stood up straight, or what she thought was straight. The whole world seemed to be tilting around her, and she didn't know which was up and which was down. "That's right," she heard herself saying. "The nuthouse."

The lights changed to green. "I'm sorry," the cabbie said, pulling away. "I just had a radio call."

Barbara crossed the street. She felt as exposed and naked as if her clothes had all been ripped off. She was trembling uncontrollably, and she was rapidly approaching the point of total panic, when she wouldn't be able to function as a person any longer. She would simply drop to the ground and shake until someone was interested enough to call an ambulance. It had happened before.

I'm sorry, Dr. Ross, I just couldn't make it. I'm sorry I let you down.

Another taxi passed, and she hailed it with an arm as stiff and mechanical as a railroad signal. The taxi stopped, drew into the curb and waited for her.

"Where to, lady?" asked the driver. A young black man with reflecting sunglasses. There were dancing dollies hanging from his rear-view mirror, and reggae music filled the cab.

Barbara climbed unsteadily into the back seat. "Eleven Argyle Street," she whispered.

"What you say? Eleven where?"

"Argyle Street," she said, as loudly and bravely as she could.

"Okay, lady," said the driver. "You're as good as there."

He spun the wheel, and the taxi skittered across the street in a U-turn. Then he drove south to the next intersection, and turned left against a red light toward the park. Barbara sat back in her seat with her eyes closed. She didn't mind how fast or violently he drove. The sooner she was safe inside a building, with the doors closed and the world shut out, the sooner she would start to feel like a human being again.

She knew Dr. Ross would be disappointed. She was sorry that she was such a failure. But he still had Henry and Bubba and Laura and Johnny, and they were all doing well. Maybe she just wasn't the type to respond to this particular kind of treatment. Maybe she didn't have enough—what did they call it in those war movies —moral fiber.

The taxi reached Shakespeare Garden, U-turned again and parked outside of Dr. Ross's apartments, its suspension bucking with the sudden stop.

"How much do I owe you?" asked Barbara, shakily.

"Buck-twenty-five. You okay?"

"Okay?"

"You look kind of spaced out, that all."

She forced herself to smile. "I just had an unpleasant experience, I guess."

The cab driver counted out her change. "It happens to everyone, once in a while. No need to let it get you upset."

"No," she said. "I suppose not."

She was reluctant to climb out of the taxi, but she knew she had to. It was so warm in here, and the music blotted out any thought of what was outside. The cab driver said, "Have a good day," and waited for her to go.

She hesitated. She made no attempt to open the door. The cab driver looked back at her and said, "Anything wrong? Did I give you the right change?"

"Yes," she said. "But I was wondering if you could do me a favor."

"Sure. What is it?"

"Would you just walk me across the sidewalk to the front door? My legs are feeling shaky."

"Okay. You just hold on."

The young driver got out of his cab, came around and opened the door for her. She felt the sudden rush of cold air, as if she was about to step out of an airlock into space. The driver took her arm, and with the odd halting gait of someone close to the very edge of their endurance and their mental strength, she slowly made her way to the front steps of Dr. Ross's apartments.

She gave the cab driver three dollars. "That's for stopping, and for caring, and for helping," she said.

He looked at her. He wore a silver crucifix in one earlobe, which swung and shone in the afternoon light. "Grandma's a mystic," he said. "She got the second sight. She say that sometimes you see people close to great danger, and you have to help them. Sometimes your help save them, sometimes it don't. But you always got to try."

"What's your name?" she asked him.

"Clarence," he said.

"Well, Clarence, I thank you," she told him, and she held the sleeve of his windbreaker for a moment as if she was really sorry to see him go.

From her bench across the street, with her paper discarded beside her and her hands thrust deep into the pockets of her coat, Dr. Alice Toland watched Barbara climb the steps of 11 Argyle Street and ring the bell. She stood up again, and shaded her eyes against the gray brightness of the afternoon.

Barbara stood in front of the door with her back to the street, concentrating her vision on the polished brass numerals "11." Don't look up, she told herself, and don't look back. She heard Clarence toot his horn as he drove away, but she didn't take her eyes off those numbers.

After a long wait, the door eventually opened. A short fat woman in a flowery apron looked out at Barbara and said, "Yes? What is it you're wanting?"

"I'm looking for—Dr. Ross," Barbara said. Her mouth felt as if it was full of ashes.

"Oh, then you must be Barbara Grey," said Mrs. Casey. "Dr. Ross told me you might be coming. Why don't you step right in?"

Barbara walked into the hallway, and felt a deep sense of relief as Mrs. Casey closed the door on the outside world.

"Dr. Ross lives on the third floor," said Mrs. Casey. "He said you could go up and wait for him until he gets back."

"Gets back? I don't understand. Isn't he there?"

"He had a game this afternoon. You know, the ice hockey. Now there's a terrible rough how-d'you-do for you, the ice hockey. All those fellows beating the devil out of each other with sticks. Go up, that's right, and you'll find Dr. Ross's place on the second landing, on the left."

"Thank you," said Barbara, trying to lick the dryness from her lips. "Do you think he's going to be long?"

"Not more than an hour, I shouldn't think. Now would you like a cup of tea while you're waiting? I was thinking of having one myself."

"I'd like that."

"Well, get on up with you then, and I'll see you in just a moment."

Barbara slowly climbed the stairs while Mrs. Casey stood in the hallway and watched her. At the first turning, Barbara looked back down at Mrs. Casey and managed an uneven smile, and Mrs. Casey gave her a wave of the hand and went off to her kitchen to brew up a pot of tea. Didn't the poor girl look absolutely terrible. White as a ghost, and shaking. No wonder Dr. Ross had her up at the nuthouse, although weren't there plenty of times with Mr. Casey when she felt like taking a place up there herself, what with his drinking and all.

Barbara found the door to Dr. Ross's apartment and opened it. She called, "Dr. Ross?" softly, just in case he was still there. Then she stepped inside and closed the door behind her.

It was strange, entering someone else's apartment when they weren't around. Especially with that huge, black and white blow-up of Dr. Ross on the kitchenette wall, watching her wherever she went. Barbara walked cautiously across the living room, trying not to disturb anything, and looked out of the window. The world

seemed far less hostile now that it was closed away
behind doors and double glazing.

She picked up one or two magazines, and then let
them drop back on the table again. She went and took
a closer look at some framed photographs of Dr. Ross
in his student days at Santa Cruz. Then there was a
framed letter from Professor Walters, of the Institute
of Motivational Therapy, congratulating Dr. Ross for
"some of the most inspired and original work I have
had the pleasure to see in a decade."

She picked up one or two ice-hockey trophies, and a
small silver cup for basketball. She put them down
again.

Her eye was caught by the gray steel filing cabinet
in the corner. She peered at it for a moment, then
stepped closer. She read the names on the white card
labels—BARBARA GREY, BERNARD KING, JOHN VENUTI,
LAURA ADAMS, HENRY LAWSON. She'd never seen her
own file, or any of the detailed reports on her progress.
She wondered why Dr. Ross had been so convinced
that she was ready to go out—what her tests had shown
about her personality and about her phobia.

She laid her hand on the metal handle. She shouldn't
really look. But Mrs. Casey was downstairs making tea,
and Dr. Ross himself wouldn't be back for an hour. So
why not? Perhaps she'd discover something about herself which would help her to get better.

The explosion was so sudden and so devastating that
she wasn't aware of anything. It filled the room with
total air pressure and total sound, and literally blew
Barbara Grey inside out. Her blood was slapped against
the opposite wall in an array of comic-book exclama-
tion marks, and her ragged, gory body was hurled behind the sofa.

It was only after the first expansion of pressure that
there was an audible, ear-splitting bang, and a sound

like the ringing of the bells of hell, which was glass windows falling into the street. The whole apartment was thick with smoke, and the drapes were blazing.

Mrs. Casey heard the explosion on the second floor. She dropped her tea tray in fright, and rushed up the last flight of stairs. There wasn't any need for her to open the apartment door, because it had been blown down to the end of the landing already. The poor old woman peered in at the smoke, her mouth open in fear, and saw so much blood that she thought a gallon of red paint had been tipped over. Then she started screaming and she couldn't stop.

By the time Mrs. Casey had reached the doorway, Dr. Alice Toland was already halfway across the street, dodging the traffic. She ran through the shattered glass on the sidewalk and up the front steps, fishing in her pocketbook for her keys. She took them out, held them up to pick the right one, and then opened the front door.

What am I doing? she thought. *I can't do this. Whatever's happened, this is the last place I ought to be.* She hesitated one more second, and then she slammed the door shut again and hurried off.

From the upstairs window she heard Mrs. Casey calling, "Will you fetch the ambulance? For the love of God, will you fetch the ambulance? There's a girl lying dead up here!"

A crowd was already gathering outside of Number 11, and as Dr. Toland turned her car around and headed north again, she heard the first whooping and warbling of sirens.

8

THE LOCKER ROOM was bursting with noise. Shouting, laughter and someone trying to sing *The Barber of Seville* in the wrong key. All around there was steam and water and hairy masculine bodies, and that hilarious horsing-around atmosphere that comes from winning a good hard game by two fantastic goals.

Peter Ross was almost dressed, and he was just raking a comb through his curls when a barrage of hoots and wolf-whistles told him that Jenny had dropped in to see him.

Ignoring the noise, she came across to Dr. Ross, put her arms around him and kissed him.

"You were fantastic," she said. "That last goal was something else. A perfect slap-shot."

"I do try to be perfect." Dr. Ross smiled, kissing her back. "Of course it comes easier to some people than it does to others."

Jenny St. Clair was slim and petite, with blond hair that was almost as curly as Dr. Ross's. She had a sharp, intelligent face, and wide bright eyes. At a guess, one probably would have thought she was an exceptionally pretty teacher, or maybe a tennis player. In fact, Jenny St. Clair was a sculptress, and an exceptionally talented one too. Her major bronze abstract *Coming Home* was on permanent display outside the Children's Hospital on Shaker Boulevard, and she was already working on a family group for the Cleveland Shore Commission.

She was independent, outspoken and free. Everything that Alice Toland wasn't. And that was why Dr. Ross liked her so much.

"Listen," she said, "I only dropped in to say that I have to go downtown to pick up some more materials. But if you want to call by in an hour . . ."

"That sounds terrific. I have to check with the hospital anyway, to see how Barbara managed."

"Oh, yes. It was Barbara's day out today, wasn't it?"

Dr. Ross raised his hand, with his fingers crossed. "If everything went well, she should be back at the hospital by now."

One of Dr. Ross's teammates came by, a big crew-cut Canadian with an Adidas bag slung over his shoulder. "That was a great shot, Doc," he said, slapping Dr. Ross on the back. "A few more games like that and we might even take home the amateur cup. How are you, Jenny?"

"I'm fine. In fact, I'm very happy. We won, didn't we?"

"We sure did," said the Canadian. "But then the doc's a very lucky man, isn't he? Off the ice, as well as on."

"Thanks for the compliment." Jenny smiled.

Dr. Ross buttoned up his coat and said, "Get going, Pearson, before I lay you out. All six-feet-nine of you."

Jenny gave Dr. Ross a quick kiss. "I have to go now. But I'll see you later, okay?"

"I'll be there," said Dr. Ross. "You can start warming up some of that French coffee for me."

Jenny left the locker room, and the doors swung behind her. As they rebounded, a security guard in a peaked cap came in and called, "Dr. Peter Ross? Is

Dr. Peter Ross still here? There's an emergency call on the telephone."

Dr. Ross glanced at his teammates, and then hurriedly pushed his way across the locker room. "I'm Dr. Ross," he told the security guard. "Where's the phone?"

The security guard led him along the concrete-floored corridor. At the far end, close to the gates which led up to the ice rink, there was a red wall phone, its receiver still dangling.

"Did they say who was calling?" asked Dr. Ross, as he walked quickly along beside the security guard.

"Police, I think," said the guard. "But they said it was real urgent."

Dr. Ross grabbed the swinging receiver and picked it up. "This is Dr. Ross," he said. "You have a call for me?"

He didn't recognize the voice at first. It sounded drier and more collected than usual. Maybe that was the way policemen always reacted when there was a crisis. While everybody else went to pieces, they shifted into cold, calm and neutral.

"There's been an accident at your apartment, Dr. Ross."

"An accident? What do you mean? Who is this?"

"This is Captain Barnes, Doctor. Your friendly neighborhood detective. I'm afraid to say that there's been a serious explosion in your living room, and that a woman has died."

"A woman?" he asked hoarsely. "What woman? Was she young, old—what?"

Captain Barnes paused for a significant moment. Then, as if he was reading from a notebook, he said, "A preliminary check in her pocketbook indicates that she was Mrs. Barbara Hudson Grey, and that she was an inmate of your phobia therapy program at Lakeshore Hospital, out on special day-release."

"Oh, Christ," said Dr. Ross. "Not Barbara."

"Would you come around to the precinct right away, please?" asked Captain Barnes. "You understand that I have to ask you some questions. And perhaps you'd be good enough to identify the body."

Dr. Ross nodded, and then he whispered, "Yes. I'll be right down."

He held the receiver up for a second or two, and then he carefully replaced it on its cradle. The security guard, watching him, asked, "Bad news, huh?"

"Bad," said Dr. Ross.

The guard shifted uncomfortably from one foot to the other. "I'm sorry," he said. "Is there anything I can—"

"No, no. Nothing," said Dr. Ross. "Thanks, but nothing."

9

CAPTAIN BARNES LOOKED as if he had been waiting for him. He was sitting behind his battered steel desk, his blunt hands together in an unconscious imitation of prayer, his eyes fixed on the door. When Dr. Ross came in and glanced around the office, he said, "Sit down, will you?" and inclined his head toward the last vacant chair.

Dr. Ross hesitated and then slowly sat down. Opposite him, sitting up straight-backed and silent, was Dr. Alice Toland. They looked at each other, but there was no communication between them—none of that intimate semaphore that real friends exchange when they find themselves in an awkward situation. Dr. Toland turned away.

Standing against the wall, half-concealed by the glare of Captain Barnes's desk lamp, was Sergeant Wheeler, a dark-haired heavily-built detective with dense eyebrows and more teeth than his mouth seemed to be able to handle. Dr. Ross had seen him before, the last time that Captain Barnes had come to visit the phobia unit. He had a line in feeble jokes, and obviously saw himself as Barnes's successor when the time came for the captain's retirement.

In a harsh, carrot-shredding voice, Captain Barnes asked, "Been to the morgue?"

Sergeant Wheeler said, "Yes, Captain."

"And—uh—identify the remains?"

"Yes, sir."

Dr. Ross said nothing, but rubbed at his face with his hand. Dr. Toland said, "Peter? Are you all right?"

Dr. Ross nodded. Yes, he was all right, if all right meant just about sane and just about able to keep his pregame sandwiches down. He'd heard the morgue assistants talking about the damage to his apartment, and about some of the bomb injuries they'd seen before, but he still hadn't been prepared for the armless, lopsided ruin of Barbara's body. Her head had been grotesquely distorted, and he knew that the ludicrous horror of it was going to haunt him for the rest of his life.

Captain Barnes said, "Dr. Toland drove over to your apartment when they told her about the explosion at the hospital. She was very good with Mrs. Casey. Calmed her down. She wanted to come back and wait for you here."

Dr. Ross said nothing. He could still remember Alice sitting on the stairs.

Barnes turned his revolving chair around and stood up. "You look like you could use a drink," he said. "I remember I did, the first time I saw a bomb victim."

Dr. Ross shook his head. His stomach was on the verge of heaving as it was. A glass of brandy would have come straight back up.

Alice Toland said, "Peter, are you sure? You're looking awfully pale."

He looked up at her, and when she saw the expression in his eyes, she raised her hands in a gesture that meant, *Okay, I was only trying to be sympathetic.* The small conflict between them wasn't lost on Captain

Barnes, who stood watching them both with his hands in his pockets, jingling his keys.

Captain Barnes was one of the last of the old Cleveland hard-liners. A man who had been trained on the streets, and who knew all about violence and innocence, confidence tricks and sudden death. When he was twenty-three, his partner had had his head blown off with a sawed-off shotgun, spraying Barnes with blood and pellets. When he was thirty, he had broken a ring of drug smugglers who were bringing in heroin from Windsor to Cleveland by private boat, and he had been shot in the thigh during the arrest. He was fifty-four now—dogged, scrupulous and tough. Cropped hair, washed-out eyes and a dark suit that could have fitted a small sofa.

The walls of Captain Barnes's office told what he was as much as anything. They were bare, except for three police posters and a notice board. On the notice board were three timetables, a duty roster and a list of internal telephone numbers. Even Barnes's desk was clear, with the single exception of a framed photograph of his wife who was smiling vaguely out at the empty office.

Captain Barnes walked around behind Dr. Ross's chair, still jingling his keys.

"Know somebody who might try to knock you off, Dr. Ross?" he asked.

Dr. Ross turned around. "Knock *me* off? What are you talking about?"

"I'm speculating," said Barnes. "I'm speculating that whoever planted that bomb wasn't really trying to kill Mrs. Barbara Grey at all."

"You mean it was put there for me?"

"Who else? I can't think of anybody having a motive for killing Mrs. Casey, can you?"

"But why the hell should anyone want to kill *me?*"

persisted Dr. Ross. "I'm just a research therapist. What harm did I ever do?"

Captain Barnes tugged at his ear and grimaced. "You did quite a heaping helping, as a matter of fact. This is what I tried to point out to the Commissioner when we were first reviewing this whole cockamamie program of yours, this phobia project, and this is exactly the kind of thing I was afraid of."

"I still don't understand."

"Think about it, Dr. Ross. Every one of those criminal white rats of yours is guilty of homicide or manslaughter."

"They're *patients,* Captain," interjected Dr. Ross. "Not white rats."

"Well, whatever. Every one of them killed somebody, and what you have to remember is that victims, as well as murderers, have friends and relatives. I've talked to some of those friends and relatives. I've had letters from them, begging me to intervene and stop your program dead. Because how do you think *you'd* feel, Dr. Ross, if the cold-blooded murderer of one of your loved ones was suddenly sprung from the penitentiary and treated like a pampered convalescent?"

Captain Barnes walked across to the opposite wall, and stood facing the chipped cream paint as if it was an audience at a police lecture.

"You may be considered the golden boy of criminal psychology among your own private circle of head-shrinkers, Dr. Ross, but in the wider circle of decent human society, where people expect criminals to be punished for their crimes, and to stay behind bars when they're put there, your name stands for everything that's gone wrong with the penal system since they first invented parole."

Dr. Ross slowly raised his head. He had difficulty

in controlling his voice. "Is that your official attitude, Captain Barnes?"

Captain Barnes turned around. "It's not an attitude, Dr. Ross. It's a fact. An official fact. Right now, I can think of twenty people who might have been responsible for planting that bomb in your apartment, at least a third of whom had the opportunity, and at least a sixth of whom had the necessary expertise."

"A sixth of twenty is three and one-third," said Dr. Ross.

"You think that's funny?" barked Captain Barnes. "You think that dead girl down there is an object of light amusement? That corpse could have been you, wise guy, with a ticket on your big toe and half your insides on the wallpaper. You just think about it."

"I am thinking about it," Dr. Ross snapped back. "And what I'm thinking is that you're purposely using this homicide inquiry to support your own personal prejudice against the phobia program. Listen—I knew there'd be opposition from the victims' relatives. I knew there might even be personal risks. But the aim of the project is far more important than any of that opposition and any of those risks. If I can find a way to cure serious phobias before their sufferers go out on the streets and start killing people out of sheer irrational fear, then I'm going to be saving a whole lot of lives in the future, and there'll be hundreds of relatives who won't ever have to go through grief and bereavement at all."

"Dr. Ross," said Captain Barnes, "I think you're forgetting something. A girl died today because of you. Doesn't that faze you at all?"

Dr. Ross looked down at his hands, clasped together in his lap. "I cared for Barbara," he said. "I cared for her, and I looked after her. She looked up to me, you know, as if I was her father or something. She relied on me. I *am* fazed, Captain Barnes, if that's what you want to know. I'm distressed and I'm angry. But I want us to keep the perspective right. If I cancel the program now, because of this, then Barbara's death will have been wasted."

Captain Barnes came over to Dr. Ross, and leaned his face very close, only about a half-inch away. Dr. Ross could see the pits in his skin, and smell a cheap supermarket-brand aftershave.

"I'm only going to say this once," murmured Captain Barnes, "but I just want you and I to know where we stand. I think that you're a fake."

The detective stood up again and smiled, and then walked back around his desk. He nodded at Dr. Ross as if to say, *That's right. No matter what the rest of the world thinks of you, that's what I believe. Now, what are you going to do about it?*

Dr. Ross said, "Is that all you're going to ask me?"

"You were at the ice rink all afternoon, in front of hundreds of people. You want me to ask you if you have an alibi?"

Just then, the door of the office was banged open, and Jenny burst in. Dr. Ross got to his feet, and she came rushing across the room into his arms. She was white-faced, and her makeup was streaked down her cheeks.

"Oh, Peter! Oh, God! At first I thought it was you! I waited and waited and when you didn't come I called your apartment. Some policeman answered and told me there'd been an explosion, somebody killed. He wouldn't even say who it was."

Dr. Ross held her close for a moment, and then took out a handkerchief and wiped her eyes for her.

"I'm okay," he said huskily. "It was Barbara. Some kind of a bomb."

"They told me outside. Oh, God, I was so frightened."

Captain Barnes watched this performance impassively. Then he said, "Find me an extra chair, will you, Wheeler? Won't you sit down, Miss . . . ?"

"St. Clair," said Dr. Ross. "Jennifer St. Clair. The well-known sculptress, if you'd have known anything at all about art."

"I know about art," said Captain Barnes quietly. "You sculpted *Coming Home,* didn't you, Miss St. Clair, and that nice piece in the lobby of the Garfield Hotel?"

"That's right," said Jenny uncertainly. Dr. Ross turned his head away in annoyance.

"You, er, you may not have met Dr. Ross's associate from the Lakeshore—Dr. Toland?" Captain Barnes asked Jenny.

Dr. Toland leaned forward in her chair and mouthed a hello. "I've seen your work," she said. "Peter and I went to one of your exhibitions last year. He even bought me one of your smaller sculptures. I forget what the occasion was."

Jenny frowned and looked up at Dr. Ross. "That's nice," she said to Dr. Toland, but without taking her eyes off Peter. "I'm pleased."

Dr. Ross remained expressionless, but he laid his hand on the back of Jenny's chair in an unmistakably proprietorial gesture.

Captain Barnes said, "I don't really have many more questions at this stage. I'm still waiting for a report from pathology, and the explosives boys have a long way to go. But I would like to know if anyone else has access to your apartment, Dr. Ross. Apart from Mrs. Casey, of course."

Dr. Ross shook his head. "The only key is mine."

"Okay," said Captain Barnes. "Now tell me this— why should Barbara Grey go to your apartment this afternoon at all?"

"I told her to go there only if she needed me desperately. Otherwise, she was supposed to make her own way back to the hospital. You know why she was out—you saw all the release papers yourself. Barbara was a chronic agoraphobe, and we believed that she was ready to go out and relate to the outside world."

"That's fair enough," Captain Barnes nodded. "But even if she *had* needed you desperately—and by the very fact that she went around to your apartment, it would seem likely that she *did*—you wouldn't have been there, would you? You were out at the ice-hockey match."

Dr. Ross held his wrist up. "When I dropped Barbara off, I thought it was much earlier than it actually was. I thought I was going to have a couple of clear hours to tidy up my notes at home. As it was, I found out when I got back there that it was almost time to go to the game."

"So what arrangements did you make for Barbara?"

"I told Mrs. Casey to take care of her. She's a reliable woman, Mrs. Casey, and as long as Barbara was inside, and not out on the streets, she shouldn't have had any problems."

Captain Barnes perched himself on the edge of his desk.

"Mrs. Casey said that when Barbara Grey rang at the door, she was hysterical. We've also located a taxi driver who took her there, a young black named"—he checked a paper on his desk—"Clarence Nodes. He said in his own words that she was acting weird, and that she had the feeling of death about her."

Sergeant Wheeler came in with an extra chair, but Dr. Ross didn't sit down. "I'd like to know what you're driving at," he asked Captain Barnes. "You have two witnesses who say that Barbara was hysterical, but no witnesses, expert or otherwise, who can give you any idea why. I know for a fact that Barbara was ready to go out and take a walk on her own. I can show you the charts, the pattern of vital responses, everything. She was ready—and that suggests to me that something else might have made her hysterical."

"You're guessing," said Captain Barnes dryly.

"Isn't that exactly what you're doing?"

"No, Dr. Ross, it isn't. I speculate, but I never guess. I'm not that kind of policeman. I have two independent witnesses who say that Barbara Grey was badly spooked and that's enough for me. It may not have much bearing on the homicide case but it does back up what I've been saying about your therapy program."

"That's totally unfair," put in Dr. Alice Toland. "Peter's work is exciting and it's important."

Captain Barnes ignored her and turned to Jenny. "Did you know any of Dr. Ross's white rats, Miss St. Clair? All right, all right—*patients?*"

Jenny shook her head. "I've seen a photograph of them, that's all."

"Well, that's a pity," said Captain Barnes. "I was hoping I could call on your feminine intuition to illuminate what might have happened. Our Dr. Toland is a little too close to the subject. A little too *partisan,* shall we say?"

Jenny wasn't sure what Captain Barnes meant, but she looked at Dr. Toland awkwardly, and then frowned again at Peter.

Captain Barnes stood up. "I don't think I need to keep any of you any longer. But I want to say one thing, Dr. Ross, before you go. Whoever rigged your file cabinet didn't do it as a practical joke. They meant to kill someone, and that someone was probably you. You wait until you see how the morning papers write it up. 'Cure-the-Killers Doctor Is Target for Mad

Bomber.' Then you may begin to understand how serious this is."

"How about my apartment?" asked Dr. Ross.

"Right at the moment it looks like the morning after the Battle of Gettysburg. It's sealed off, too. You got someplace to stay?"

"My place," said Jenny, in a voice that had a touch of challenge in it.

Dr. Ross said, "I'll take Miss St. Clair home. After that, you can either call my answering service or the hospital. They'll contact me through my bleeper."

He opened his coat to show Captain Barnes the small electronic paging device clipped to his belt.

"All right," said Captain Barnes. "Meanwhile, I suggest you exercise a modest amount of discretion before you open any doors or boxes or files. And if you suspect anything—letters or packages in particular —then I want you to call me straight away."

He took out a half-burned cigar and clenched it between his teeth. "I don't agree with what you're doing, Dr. Ross, but I have to defend your right to stay alive. I hope you don't mind my paraphrasing Voltaire."

Dr. Ross gave the detective an odd look, and then ushered Jenny out of the room. He didn't even say goodbye to Dr. Alice Toland, who sat in her chair long after he had gone, her back straight, her knees together and an expression on her face that could have been determination but most probably was nothing but sadness.

Captain Barnes said gently, "Do you need a ride anywhere, Dr. Toland?" but she shook her head.

10

JENNY LIVED IN an old building not far from the Cleveland Zoo. It stood in a short street of iron-framed Victorian houses which a series of fortunate accidents of planning and development had left standing, and which had now become a small artistic community of their own. There was a famous watercolor painter living next door at Number 9, and a cellist with the Cleveland Symphony Orchestra could often be heard practicing Dvorak from Number 5.

He was playing his cello tonight as they got out of Dr. Ross's Porsche and crossed the sidewalk. Sad, elegant music that seemed to crystallize in the chilly evening air, like molten sugar spun into cold water.

Jenny said, "Can you hear that? Isn't it weepy?"

"Weepy?" asked Dr. Ross, as if he didn't know what the word meant.

She took his arm. "You're shattered. I'm sorry. Come on up and have a drink."

They went into the darkened lobby, and Jenny switched on the light. There was an old elevator at the end of the hall, with trellis gates and brass handles, but as they walked toward it they could see that it had resolutely positioned itself between the first and the second floors.

"Stuck again," said Jenny, shaking her head. "How about some exercise before your drink?"

"Looks like I don't have any choice."

Without speaking, they climbed the stairs to Jenny's fourth-floor apartment. Their footsteps echoed around the brown-tiled walls and down the empty elevator shaft. When they reached the top, Jenny unlocked her front door and pushed it open.

Even though it was night, the apartment was unnaturally bright. The light came from a huge glass skylight in the roof, which gave them a glittering view of downtown Cleveland and beyond, across the misty gray expanse of Lake Erie. Underneath the skylight stood three of Jenny's latest pieces, all in various stages of completion. Two abstract blocks in stainless steel joined together by a copper shaft. A life-sized nude in bronze. A stylized figure 7 for the executive offices of the Seven Seas Corporation in Seattle.

Jenny put down her bag and walked across to the kitchen area, which was built on a raised platform at the far end of the studio. There was a thick butcher-block table, an old-fashioned iron range decorated with blue and white ceramic tiles and a row of burnished copper pans. She opened a pine cupboard and took down two glasses and a bottle of whiskey. Dr. Ross slowly tugged off his coat, with all the stiffness of a man who has been shaken up in a near-fatal auto accident, and sat down

Jenny cracked ice from the Frigidaire, dropped it into the glasses, topped them up with whiskey and handed one to Peter Ross without a word. He sipped the liquor slowly, and then he leaned back in his chair and let out a long breath of relief.

"I feel like I've failed," he said in a tired voice. "I really feel like I've failed."

"How have you failed?" asked Jenny. "You couldn't have known about that bomb. It wasn't your fault."

"But if Barbara had been okay, she would have gone straight back to the hospital. . . ."

"Darling, she probably *was* okay. I know that Captain Barnes said she was hysterical. But maybe she was just excited. Maybe she just wanted to tell you how well she'd managed."

"I'd like to believe that," said Dr. Ross dully. "Unfortunately, I don't think I can. Barbara came around to see me because she needed my help. She wasn't ready to go out on her own. And now she's dead."

"But the bomb was meant for you, not her."

"Do you think that makes me feel any less responsible?"

"I'm not saying it should. But who on earth would want to kill you? Do you really believe it was some angry relative? That seems pretty farfetched to me. Why didn't they do it before, when it was first announced that you were going to run this project? I don't believe people stay angry for as long as that, do you?"

"I don't know," said Dr. Ross. "I just can't work it out."

"Do you think it could be someone from the hospital? Someone who's jealous of your work? Dr. Clemens, for instance?"

He looked up and then shook his head in unhappy amusement. "I can't imagine poor old Dr. Clemens planting a bomb for the life of me. Sure, she's caustic. But she's not a terrorist type. She wouldn't know plastic explosive from putty."

"Then maybe one of the other patients did it? They're killers, aren't they? Maybe one of them feels you're pushing too hard and wants to stop you."

"That won't wash, either," said Dr. Ross, finishing his whiskey with one shivering swallow and putting the glass down on the kitchen stairs. "They all trust me and respect me, and I'd know straight away if any one of them felt hostile."

Jenny sat down on the stairs beside him and hugged her knees, the way Barbara had in the car.

"Was there somebody you knew in California who didn't like you? Or a hockey opponent? People commit murders for the craziest reasons, you know."

Dr. Ross shook his head. "I can't think of anyone."

"You *must*. I mean—they broke into your apartment somehow. Is there anyone else with a key?"

"You heard what I told Captain Barnes."

"Sure. But what you told Captain Barnes and what my feminine intuition tells me are two different things. Actually, Captain Barnes guessed it, and he knew that I'd guessed it, and that's why he wanted my opinion."

"Guessed what? Come on, Jenny, I'm tired."

Jenny ran her finger around the rim of her glass. "Dr. Alice Toland has a key to your apartment. Isn't that right?"

Dr. Ross got up from the chair and walked cagily across the studio. He stood for a moment beside the two shiny abstract blocks, his face reflected in their polished surfaces, so that it looked as if there were two of him. Dr. Peter Ross and his mirror-image brother.

"Which piece of mine did you buy for her?" asked Jenny.

He looked away, toward his own reflection. "What do you care?" he said.

"I care," she insisted. "Which one?"

He made a brief curving gesture in the air. "The little one. *Woman Asleep*."

"I see," she said.

"What do you see?" he demanded. "I bought that before I even knew you. How can you be jealous of something that happened when we weren't even—"

"I don't know," she interrupted. Then, more softly, "I don't know. I just know that I am."

She walked across the studio toward him and stood a little way away, her hand on the narrow leg of her nude bronze. Her eyes were misted, and when she spoke her voice was scarcely audible.

"People don't understand sculpture. Because a sculpture is a physical, external object, standing on its own two feet, they don't realize that it comes out of your mind. I create a man, and everybody thinks it's a man. A being in its own right. They forget that it couldn't have existed without my inspiration."

Dr. Ross said nothing, although he lowered his eyes and looked away from her. Jenny came closer, so that her reflection joined his.

"That's why I'm jealous about *Woman Asleep*," she said. "Dr. Alice Toland used to love you, and from what I can see she still does. And yet a piece of my mind and my heart is sitting in her house right now."

"You're being ridiculous," said Dr. Ross under his breath.

"Am I? Well, maybe I am. But the only times you've ever mentioned her, I've gotten the distinct impression that she was some kind of middle-aged dragon. Why didn't you tell me about her? That you'd had an affair?"

Dr. Ross looked up at her sharply. "I didn't tell you because I knew you'd react just like this. Besides, I think it's vulgar to talk about your past relationships."

"Vulgar?"

"That's it, vulgar. And irrelevant too. Why talk about something that stopped being important months ago?"

"Peter—"

He held her wrist so tight that it hurt. "You make me happy, Jenny," he said. "Just you remember that. So let's forget about the past, hunh? Don't let's clutter up our lives with things that don't matter anymore. Please."

For a moment they stood facing each other like two statues of tension and conflict. Then Dr. Ross released Jenny's wrist and held out his arms for her, and she came up close and rested her head against his shoulder, hugging him tight.

"I'm sorry," she said. "I'm behaving like a fool."

"It's okay," he told her. "We've both had a tough day."

"It's just that I care for you so much," she said. "Somebody's threatening your life, threatening to hurt you, and I can't do anything about it. You're mine, and I want to protect you, don't you understand that?"

"Jenny," said Dr. Ross warningly.

"Stay here with me," she asked him. "Not just for tonight, but until this is all over."

A muscle flinched in his cheek. "I don't know. We'll see."

"You'll be safe here."

"Sure, I'll be safe," he said abruptly. "Wrapped up in cotton and smothered."

"Peter, what do you mean?"

He raised a hand. His fingers were stretched wide apart and they were quivering with suppressed emotion.

"I don't want to be smothered, that's all. I just don't want to be smothered."

Jenny stared at him. She had never heard him talking this way before. What did he mean by smothering? She didn't want to smother him—simply to love him and look after him. Maybe he'd had a bad experience with Dr. Toland. After all, Dr. Toland had come all the way down to the police precinct to see him and protect him, even though she had no evidence to offer.

Had she wanted to be close to Peter again? Earn his gratitude and maybe his affection?

The whole thing made Jenny feel uneasy. Particularly the fact that Dr. Toland had a key to Peter's apartment. And particularly the fact that Dr. Toland seemed to behave as if her relationship with Peter wasn't completely over—at least, not from *her* point of view.

"Peter," Jenny said gently, "we're both tired. Let's forget it for now. Would you like something to eat?"

Dr. Ross shook his head. Jenny held him in her arms and ruffled his curls. "This has hit you hard, hasn't it?"

She kissed him once, twice, three times, and then she took his hand and led him across the studio to the archway that led to her bedroom. There was a wide divan there, covered in a decorative Indian bedspread, and the walls of the room were hung with dozens of framed sketches for Jenny's sculptures. There was a gas log fire in the old Victorian hearth, and she knelt down and lit it while Dr. Ross stripped off his shirt. She turned around and looked at him appreciatively in the flickering firelight. His flat, muscular stomach. His well-developed chest. A man who cared for himself and cared about others too.

She stood up, and he drew her nearer and hugged her for a moment. Then, without a word, he unbuttoned her blouse, baring her small uptilted breasts. He placed one hand over her left breast as if he was seeking access to a secret door that only opened for palm prints. Her dark nipple rose between his fingers. He kissed her lightly and then more deeply and more searchingly. He loosened the button of her jeans and tugged them down over her hips.

Naked, she was as slim as a water nymph, and there was something magical about the way she looked in the firelight. She lay back on the durry with her blond curls shining, and Dr. Ross stripped off his pants and lay down beside her, his lips feeding silently and passionately from her neck and shoulders. Her mouth parted slightly and she began to breathe more deeply.

"Oh, Peter—" she whispered. "Oh, Peter, my darling—"

He entered her from the side and entwined his legs around hers, so that against the formalized pattern on the Indian bedspread they looked like two sensual lovers from the ancient Temple of Konarak. He thrust into her harder and harder, and his right hand clutched at her breasts until he was leaving marks in the flesh.

For Jenny, his fierceness was partly arousing and partly frightening. She could hear him grinding his teeth as he came closer and closer to a climax, and his gasps of exertion were almost like sobs. Before tonight his lovemaking had always been gentle, considerate and athletic. Now he was treating her body like the object of some pent-up rage. It was the closest thing to rape she had ever experienced.

He made a hoarse, inarticulate noise, but as he climaxed he slipped out of her, either deliberately or accidentally, and his semen went across the bedspread. Jenny lay there beside him, quivering and unsatisfied, her muscles so tense that she could scarcely breathe.

Dr. Ross said, "I'm sorry."

She pressed her forehead close to his. "No," she said. "Don't ever be sorry. You've had a bad time today. You love me, and that's good enough."

She sat up. "I'm going to fix us another drink. Why don't you close your eyes for a while and get some rest?"

He turned toward the fire. The flames were reflected as hot dancing pinpoints in his eyes. "Yes," he said, in a drowsy voice, "I guess I might at that."

Jenny took her Japanese robe from the peg beside the door and wrapped it around her. By the time she reached the archway and turned around to look at Dr. Ross, he was asleep, with one hand clenched like a child.

Some men are so strange, she thought. They drive themselves and everybody around them like charioteers in Ben Hur, and if they stumble or falter, they feel like it's the end of the world.

She went back across the bedroom, loosened the durry and covered his naked body. He murmured in his sleep as if he was having a bad dream.

11

THE NEWSMEN WERE waiting for him outside the hospital the following morning, huddled under their wet raincoats like a sorry group of buzzards. He parked his car in the space marked DR. ROSS, switched off the windshield wipers and climbed out. He heard one of the newsmen say, "That's him!" and they all started to cross the puddly parking lot toward him.

"Hi, Dr. Ross," said one of them, a short gingery man with a rain-spotted notebook. "I'm Evans from the *Plain Dealer*. Can you tell us how you're feeling this morning?"

"I'm fine," said Dr. Ross.

"That was a pretty narrow escape, though, wasn't it? If you'd have come back to your apartment before the girl did . . ."

Dr. Ross shrugged. "I can't really talk about it now. I have to report to Dr. Clegg. Now, if you'll excuse me . . ."

He started walking across the parking lot and the newsmen hurried after him. A photographer in a wet green fedora danced along sideways and took as many pictures as he could.

"Do you think this could be some kind of vendetta

against you, because of your work with killers?" asked
another reporter.

"If it is, it's a very sadly mistaken vendetta," said
Dr. Ross. "Each one of my patients is a volunteer—
someone who has offered to help me cure his psychological condition of his own free will. And *her* free
will too, of course. There are two women in the course.
Or, at least, there were."

"Are you going to think twice about continuing the
project?" asked the sandy-haired newsman.

Dr. Ross paused at the hospital steps. "That kind of
decision isn't mine to make. I'll abide by whatever Lakeshore decides and whatever Townsend Cereals decides.
But I'd just like to remind you gentlemen that psychological pioneers like Freud and Jung and therapists
like Masters and Johnson were all reviled in their own
time, and that as far as I'm concerned the measure of
public reaction is the measure of success.

"If I can successfully cure chronic phobias, then
there is no question at all that I will have made the
most significant contribution to criminal psychotherapy
in twenty years."

Just then, the rain-beaded doors of the hospital
opened, and Captain Barnes appeared, wearing a
crumpled raincoat with damp shoulders. "Are you coming in?" he asked Dr. Ross. "Or are you spending the
rest of the morning with your press corps?"

The reporters turned away from Dr. Ross like a
troupe of seals who have suddenly been offered a fresh
bucket of fish. "Captain Barnes—" they entreated.
"Captain Barnes, do you have any leads yet?"

"All in good time," said Captain Barnes harshly.
"Are you coming, Dr. Ross?"

"Sure," said Dr. Ross, and nodded to the newsmen.
"Maybe I'll see you guys later."

"Hold it right there," said a photographer. "That's it—smile!"

Captain Barnes gave the lensman a sour grimace and ushered Dr. Ross into the building. "I've been waiting for you since eight forty-five," he said, looking around him as he walked.

"I don't usually get here till nine-thirty," Dr. Ross told him. "I thought you would have known that."

They both hesitated outside the swing doors of the Titus E. Frobisher wing, but then Dr. Ross pushed a door open for Captain Barnes and said, "Go ahead, Captain. Age before beauty."

"We got our report on the bomb," said Captain Barnes as he walked along the echoing, dimly lit corridor.

"And?"

Captain Barnes paused by the severe portrait of Titus E. Frobisher. "What did Gerry Ford say once? 'If that man was alive today, he'd roll over in his grave.' "

"The bomb," Dr. Ross prompted him.

"Oh, sure. The bomb. Well—there's no doubt about it at all. The filing cabinet was a carefully prepared booby trap."

"Then it *was* for me," said Dr. Ross.

Captain Barnes looked back at him over his damp, raincoated shoulder. "Oh, yes," he said with a lopsided smile. "It was definitely for you."

"But you still have no clues about who or why?"

"I can reason out *why*. I can't yet deduce *who*. But it wasn't an expert. The booby trap was wired up according to the instructions in U.S. Army explosives manuals, but it wasn't done by a veteran. A veteran would have used far less explosive, and probably would have sited the plastic inside of the drawer, instead of outside, to cause the most localized shrapnel injury."

They passed the open doors of Bubba's room, Johnny's room, Henry's room. Dr. Ross glanced in each of them as he passed, but the three criminals, aware that he was accompanied by the law, were all studiously managing to look the other way. They could smell police like they could smell prison food. Both had the same sour, sharp odor of captivity and deprivation.

Henry had once said, "The law is like Medusa. You only have to look into its eyes once, and it turns you into stone."

Dr. Ross fumbled with his keys at the door which separated the men from the women. He knew it wasn't locked, but he didn't want Captain Barnes to realize it. When they walked through, Laura was waiting by the door of her room, smoking a cigarette. Her hair was tied up in a scarf, and she was wearing a shapeless, unrevealing dress. She looked at Captain Barnes with suspicion.

"This is Laura Adams," said Dr. Ross. "Laura, say hello to Captain Barnes."

Captain Barnes kept his eyes on Dr. Ross. "She doesn't have to bother," he said coldly. "I read her file already. I'm well acquainted."

"Dr. Ross—" Laura frowned.

"It's okay, Laura," said Dr. Ross soothingly. "I just have to talk to Captain Barnes for a minute or two. Then we can start our morning group. Don't worry, huh?"

"Okay," said Laura uncertainly.

Dr. Ross and Captain Barnes walked along to the office at the end of the corridor. Sergeant Wheeler was already there, his wide bottom parked on the side of Dr. Ross's desk, flicking through a copy of *Chic*. When he saw Dr. Ross come in, he arrogantly tossed the magazine back onto the desk and stood up.

"Sergeant Wheeler," said Dr. Ross tightly, setting his briefcase down on his desk and clicking the locks open.

"Dr. Ross." The sergeant nodded.

There was a difficult pause. Then Sergeant Wheeler said, "You always allow that kind of sexual stuff in here?"

"What sexual stuff?" asked Dr. Ross.

"That magazine. You let the prisoners see that?"

"They asked me for it. Along with *Newsweek, Fortune, National Geographic* and *The New York Review of Books.* Why?"

"Bad policy, wouldn't you say?" asked Sergeant Wheeler. "Frustrated men, locked up for life. Bad policy to get them excited with that kind of stuff."

Dr. Ross picked up the magazine, peered at it for a moment and then shrugged. "From my experience, you're wrong, Sergeant. However offensive *you* may find a magazine like this, it indicates to me when my patients ask for it that they are still interested in the normal processes of human contact, both sexual and emotional. If they utterly refused to look at pictures of naked girls, then I'd really start to worry."

Sergeant Wheeler looked at Captain Barnes with an expression that could only have meant, *See what I mean? This guy's exactly what we've said he was all along. A soft-headed liberal. A lover of homicidal maniacs.*

Captain Barnes took off his hat. Dr. Ross said, "Sit down. I hate to see a detective looking uncomfortable."

Both policemen sat in the modern Italian chairs opposite his desk, and both found their suspended leather seats to be precarious and awkward. Dr. Ross remained standing, and, as Captain Barnes talked to him, he quickly and neatly tore open his mail with a paper knife.

"What I have to know now is whether you have any secret suspicions about who might have tried to kill you," said Captain Barnes. "Some old adversary from

your college times in California, perhaps? Some clever
student who never quite made it as far as you did, who
might feel jealous? Maybe a girlfriend you ditched, who
resents your new-found fame? Maybe a recent ex-
mistress?"

Dr. Ross, unfolding a letter, looked up sharply.

Captain Barnes said, "Why didn't you tell me that
Dr. Alice Toland had a key to your apartment?"

Dr. Ross looked down again. "It was personal."

"You don't think an attempt on your life is personal?"

"Listen," snapped Dr. Ross, "there is absolutely no
way that Dr. Toland—"

Captain Barnes raised his arm. Dangling from a
gold fob between his fingers was the only copy of Dr.
Ross' apartment key, as well as a front-door key to
Number 11 Argyle Street.

"I've spent the morning wandering around the hospital, just looking and listening," said Captain Barnes.
"In the end, somebody clued me in about Dr. Toland,
and all I had to do then was go directly to her office
and ask her if she had a key. She turned it over without a murmur.

"You should have told me," he added. "In a homicide case, we can't afford the luxury of personal privacy.
Nor the self-indulgence of making our own minds up
about who did it or who didn't do it."

"All right," said Dr. Ross. "So what have you
learned? That I used to go out with Dr. Toland? That
I don't any longer? What good has that done you?"

"I'm not interested in prying into your private af-
fairs," said Captain Barnes. "As a matter of fact, I
couldn't be less interested. But I'm employed by the
police department to do two things. One, to find out who
killed Barbara Grey and bring that person to justice,
and, two, to protect you from further attempts that

may be made on your life. So, since I'm employed to do those two things, I'm going to do them. And I'm not going to let your personal sensitivity stand in my way. Have you got that?"

Dr. Ross didn't answer, but slit open another letter.

"I want to make one thing plain," said Captain Barnes. "My prime suspects are these criminal white rats of yours, all four of them. Whatever treatment you've given them, they're all convicted killers, and I can tell you from plain tough first-hand experience that once a psychopathetic murderer has found that he can solve a problem by killing once, then he'll kill again."

"I'm a father figure to them," said Dr. Ross. "Why should they possibly want to kill me? If it wasn't for me, they'd all be back in prison."

"Maybe you're putting them under too much pressure. This is a pretty stiff therapy course, right? Maybe one of them can't take the strain. So—rather than flunk out, or go back to jail because he was a failure—he decides to waste you."

Captain Barnes stood up and thrust his hands deep into his raincoat pockets. "I want to tell you something," he went on. "Most of the homicides committed in the Cleveland metropolitan area are family matters. Husbands murdering wives. Wives murdering husbands. Sons murdering fathers. People are driven to kill by an overwhelming sense of rage and guilt, by a sense that they've failed and that somehow the person they want to kill has been responsible for that failure."

"You're quite the psychoanalyst," said Dr. Ross caustically.

"No, I'm not an analyst," retorted Captain Barnes. "I'm a man with years and years of bitter experience. A man who's seen more murder victims than you've seen breakfasts. Why do you think I fought so hard against this bird brained project of yours? I've seen it all for real. Not just pathology photographs and artists' impressions. I've seen what these people you've got in this maniacs' vacation home can do. And you mark my words. If they think of you as a father figure, which you say they do, then you are *statistically* more likely to be murdered by one of them."

"You're talking garbage," said Dr. Ross. "These patients—"

"These patients are convicted killers!" barked Captain Barnes. Then, realizing how loud his outburst had been, he took a deep, steadying breath and lowered his voice. "I'll make a wager with you, Dr. Ross," he said. "I've never done it with anyone before, but I'll do it now. The wager is that the person who was responsible for setting that bomb in your apartment is in this hospital wing right now."

Dr. Ross had finished with his mail. He peeled off his coat and hung it up on a peg by the door. Then he said, "You realize, of course, that all of these patients are locked in twenty-four hours a day, and that none of them has ever been missing, even for five minutes?"

"They have visitors, don't they?"

"Of course."

"And a visitor would be just as capable of setting a booby trap as the prisoner himself?"

Dr. Ross loosened his tie. "Are you seriously trying to tell me that you suspect one of my patients? One in particular?"

"I've been through all of their records."

"Who the hell—"

"Don't worry. It's all official. Dr. Clegg gave them to me last night."

"I see. And?"

"And—that's why I'm here this morning. Now that I've examined their paperwork, I'd like to see them all in the flesh."

Dr. Ross planted his hands on his hips in suppressed exasperation. He knew it was the hospital's duty to assist the police. Yet, on the other hand, it was also their clear duty to protect their patients. Whatever Captain Barnes knew his phobia sufferers to be, Dr. Ross knew them to be confused, sensitive and troubled people. People who wouldn't have dreamed of killing if their fears hadn't driven them right up against the wall.

"I'm meeting all four of them for a group discussion in a moment," said Dr. Ross. "Maybe you'd like to call by later, when I've calmed them all down about Barbara's death."

"Can't I sit in?"

"That's impossible, I'm afraid. I'm completely bound by the ethics of professional confidentiality."

Captain Barnes tiredly nodded his head. "Sure. The sacred trust between doctor and patient. I saw a TV show about that once. A psychiatrist was asked what he'd do if one of his patients confessed to a major crime. Would he betray his patient's confidence? The psychiatrist thought about it and then he said—well, do you know what he said?"

"I could make an educated guess," said Dr. Ross, irritated.

"And you'd probably be right," said Captain Barnes. " 'The best thing I could do,' said the psychiatrist, 'would be to persuade the patient to go give himself up to the police of his own accord.' "

Sergeant Wheeler gave a loud, sardonic snort. "The trouble is," he put in, "that in your particular case you couldn't persuade the criminal to give himself up, because the intended vicitim is you."

Dr. Ross put his hand over his mouth thoughtfully.

"Come on," asked Captain Barnes. "All I want to do is watch them. There won't be any breach of confidentiality. It's not like you're giving them a treatment, is it? You're just going to talk about Barbara and settle them down generally, right?"

"Well," said Dr. Ross, slowly, "I did promise Dr. Clegg that I'd try to help you in any way I could."

"I won't interrupt you," said Captain Barnes. "I won't say a single word."

Dr. Ross drummed his fingers on his desk for a while. Then he said, "All right, Captain. I'll arrange it. But I want one thing to be perfectly clear. On no account must the patients realize you're observing them. If they know that I've allowed you to watch them, then their confidence in me will be severely shaken, and it could put them back weeks."

Captain Barnes looked down at Sergeant Wheeler, who was sitting perched in his chair like an overweight parrot. Sergeant Wheeler smiled.

"That's a deal," said Captain Barnes.

12

To the four patients, the room where they met for group discussions was the warmest, safest, most relaxing room they knew. It had been divided off from the far end of the lecture hall, so that they had to pass The Box to get there. Each one of them skirted The Box as if he was afraid it might jump at him, or that the sides might suddenly fall flat and reveal inside the snakes and rapists and dizzying heights that terrified them all so much. But soon they were inside the group discussion room, and Dr. Ross had closed the door behind them, and they felt at ease.

It was a simple, modern room, decorated in neutral colors. There were six chairs, covered in pale woven fabric, and a glass-topped table. On the wall behind Dr. Ross was a mirror, in which the patients could all see themselves. The room itself made no statement at all. It wasn't pretty, or aggressive, or overly soothing. All the feelings inside it had to come from the patients themselves.

Four pairs of anxious eyes watched Dr. Ross as he sat down facing his research group and crossed his legs. They were all unsettled by the one empty chair that stood slightly apart from the others at the side of the room. Barbara's chair.

Dr. Ross said, "I talked to Dr. Clegg this morning on the telephone. He said the police can probably release Barbara's—well, they can probably arrange for Barbara to be cremated at the end of the week. We'll hold a funeral service in the Hospital Chapel, and we'll all go together."

Laura's shoulders began to shake with sobs, and tears ran down her cheeks. Henry put his arm around her and tried to calm her. Johnny, sitting back in his chair ferociously chewing gum, looked on with embarrassment.

Henry said, "I think we'd all like you to know that if there's anything we can possibly do, Dr. Ross . . . even if you want us to talk to Dr. Clegg in your favor . . . well, we're prepared to."

"Thank you, Henry," said Dr. Ross. Henry was the one he relied on most. Courteous, fiftyish, with cropped gray hair and the appearance of a slightly seedy bank clerk. Henry's shoes were always brightly polished and his frayed shirts were also given an extra pressing when they came back from the hospital laundry service. It was hard to believe that Henry had once pulled the trigger of a Colt automatic and sent a .45-caliber bullet through the chest of a young police officer, rather than jump eleven feet down to the ground.

Bubba said, "This has hit us all pretty hard, Dr. Ross. We're all really cut up about it."

Johnny nodded. "That Barbara was bright, you know? Brighter'n most of us. She didn't deserve to go out like that."

Dr. Ross raised his hand. "I know how you feel. It's been a blow to all of us. But I want to say this. The best tribute we can pay to Barbara is for all of us to work harder at the project—for all of us to make even greater efforts to overcome our fears. Because the best tribute we can pay to Barbara is to show the world that she didn't die for no reason at all. She died trying to prove that people like her, and that people like you, Johnny, and you, Henry, can all be cured."

Bubba said, "We'll try, Dr. Ross. You can count on that."

Laura, wiping her eyes with her sleeve, said, "That's right. We'll all do better. Just for her."

"And for yourselves too," said Dr. Ross quietly. "It's what she would have wanted, after all."

"What puzzles me, Dr. Ross, is who did it," put in Henry. "I mean, if it hadn't have been Barbara, who only went around to your apartment by mistake, then it would have been *you*, wouldn't it? That bomb was actually intended for you."

"Well, I sure as hell didn't plant it," said Johnny.

"Me neither," said Bubba.

Dr. Ross sat back in his chair, steepled his fingers and looked across the room at all of them. Johnny, with his early Elvis hairstyle and his constantly churning gum. Bubba, with his scarred face and his eyes that wouldn't stay still. Laura, pretty and childlike, but as vulnerable as a damaged flower. Henry, methodical and polite, an endless player of chess and backgammon and a relentless filler-in of every crossword he ever came upon. Clue 27 across: *Who wants Peter Ross dead?*

"Well," coaxed Dr. Ross. "Do any of you have any opinions?"

"About who planted the bomb?" asked Bubba. "It couldn't have been any of us, could it? Like, we're all incarcerated here."

"You all have relatives and friends," Dr Ross pointed out.

Bubba grunted in amusement and slapped his thigh. "I can just picture my buddy Charles trying to fix up something like a bomb. He tried to fix a toaster once, and all that happened was he set light to this big wide tie of his with a naked lady painted on it. Was he mad!"

Henry said, "Have you considered that it might be the relative of somebody we killed?"

Dr. Ross said nothing at all. He wanted the four of them to talk this one out for themselves. Not just for their benefit, or for his, but for the benefit of the two detectives sitting only a few feet behind him, their intent faces concealed from his patients by the two-way mirror.

In the small monitoring room behind the mirror, Captain Barnes was leaning back in his chair, watching the group discussion with a face as impassive as plain pound cake. His wet raincoat lay on the floor beside him, discarded. Sergeant Wheeler was leaning over the console which transmitted the patients' voices from the main discussion room, his face close to the glass. He reached back to scratch his backside, and Captain Barnes flicked his eyes toward him in distaste. Captain Barnes didn't say much, but he was scrupulous and fastidious, and intolerant of any kind of human weakness at all. Captain Barnes' eleven-year-old son Barney was the best damned baseball pitcher his school had ever seen, and he'd never had a dental filling in his life.

Laura's voice, distorted by the loudspeaker system, said, "I think it's someone in the hospital. One of the doctors, you know? They're all jealous of the phobia project."

Sergeant Wheeler consulted the notepad on the console in front of him. "That's Laura Adams. The one who dug the guy's eyes out with scissors."

"Charming," said Captain Barnes.

Bubba's voice boomed, "I think it's that Dr. Clegg! Have you seen that guy? He hates Dr. Ross's guts, and I know that for sure. He tries to hide it, but have you listened to the man?"

Captain Barnes grunted, and Sergeant Wheeler turned to him expectantly, but Barnes simply waved him to keep on listening.

Bubba said, "You remember that piece in *Newsweek?* The one where they said that Dr. Ross was brilliant and all? Well, that piece didn't hardly mention Dr. Clegg once, and I know for a fact that Dr. Clegg was sore about that."

"How do you know that?" demanded Johnny. "Did Dr. Clegg call you or something?"

"That Sue Ann from the canteen told me. She said she was serving up the lunch in the hospital boardroom, and Dr. Clegg was complaining about the whole phobia thing like crazy, and how Dr. Ross was getting all the credit."

Captain Barnes said dryly, "Sergeant, make a note of that. Security leak through someone called Sue Ann in the canteen. Make sure the hospital gets an official notification to change the catering staff who feed these prisoners, and then rotate them regularly."

"Yessir," said Wheeler, making notes.

Henry was saying, "I don't see how it could possibly have been Dr. Clegg. If he wanted to get back at Dr. Ross, he'd have a dozen different ways of doing it, apart from blowing him up. He could simply fire him, for beginners, or withdraw Lakeshore's support for the phobia project. I mean, Townsend may supply the finance, but Lakeshore gives us all the facilities."

"You're right, Henry," put in Dr. Ross. "Dr. Clegg doesn't really fit the bill as a homicidal bomber, does he?"

"I don't know," said Johnny. "It wouldn't surprise me if he had a couple of screws loose. Most shrinks are nuttier than the nuts, if you ask me!"

Dr. Ross grinned.

Behind the mirror Captain Barnes said, "That old guy in the gray suit. That's Henry Lawson, isn't it?"

"That's right, sir. Cop killer, that one."

"Done some time in the Army, hasn't he?"

Sergeant Wheeler checked the file. "That's right, sir. Trained at Fort Sill, Oklahoma, in field artillery. Served about six months in Korea."

"Anything else that might relate?"

"I don't know, sir. But he worked for a time for a quarrying company in New Hampshire—that was in 1958."

Captain Barnes took out a stick of chewing gum, unwrapped it, folded it in half and tucked it into his mouth.

"A quarrying company, huh? So he might know more than most about explosives? And he might well know somebody else who's something of an expert—somebody who could have let himself into Dr. Ross's apartment and fixed up his files?"

Sergeant Wheeler smirked. "If you say so, sir."

Captain Barnes nodded. "Conspiracy to murder is a serious charge, Sergeant. Especially on top of an existing life sentence. And Lawson could have a motive, too. I see from his project files that he's next to the bottom in progress, and for a conscientious man like that—well, maybe it's making him feel resentful."

"Could be, sir."

Over the monitor Laura's voice said, "What about Dr. Alice Toland? Dr. Ross left her, didn't he, and took up with a new girlfriend?"

"That's right," put in Johnny enthusiastically. "I've seen her looking at the doc, and if she don't still have the hots for him, then I'm a duck's uncle."

Bubba said, "You're right, Johnny. I've seen her, too. You remember that time she came around to see him here? She was playing it real cool, sure. Like, cold as ice. But all the time you could dig she was boiling, you know? Bubbling under. And if you ask me, it's real easy for love to turn into hate."

Henry nodded. "That's the oldest motive for murder there ever was. Jealousy, 'cruel as the grave . . .' "

Dr. Ross suddenly stood up. He knew his patients were only testing, only exploring, only allowing themselves the therapeutic luxury of speaking out loud whatever came into their minds, but enough was enough. On the other side of the mirror Captain Barnes and Sergeant Wheeler exchanged a knowing nod which meant, *See, when you start poking at their tender spots, the liberals just can't take it.*

"You're way off target," Dr. Ross snapped at his patients. "Whoever tried to kill me wanted directly or indirectly to get at *you*. That's what nobody around here seems to want to understand, even the police. Maybe they have a good reason not to."

"What do you mean, Doc?" asked Johnny, sitting up straighter.

"I mean that nobody I know of has any really sound motive for killing me except those people who want to put a stop to this program. The people who want to show that it's useless trying to cure people like you, and that I'm a failure. Now, these people include the friends and relatives of the victims of your particular crimes. They include some influential members of the prison commission. They also include some pretty senior policemen.

"The only way we can fight back is by showing those people that they're wrong—that we *are* succeeding— that we *are* overcoming your fears. They're afraid of you, as long as you remain uncured. And the collective hostility they feel toward me and you and this whole program because of their fear is as strong as anything that you've ever felt within yourselves, I can tell you."

"Maybe you should start curing *them,* not us," said Henry dolefully.

"Maybe you've got something there," agreed Dr. Ross.

There was a sharp rapping at the door. The four patients looked up, startled, and then frowned quizzically at Dr. Ross.

"It's okay," Dr. Ross told them. "It's only the police."

Captain Barnes came in, shrugging on his raincoat. While the collar was still twisted around at the back, he reached out an arm and beckoned at Henry Lawson. Henry sat up nervously, and then pointed to himself as if he couldn't believe that the detective had chosen him.

"Dr. Ross . . . ?" he said.

"It's all right, Henry," nodded Dr. Ross. "They have to talk to each of you, just as a matter of routine."

"But, Doctor, I didn't *do* anything," protested Henry. "I didn't have anything to do with it at all. I mean, how could I?"

"Henry, we're going to have to go along with them," Dr. Ross told him more firmly. "Just answer their questions, and everything will be okay. The more fuss we make, the worse it's going to be for the program."

Captain Barnes tugged his collar straight. "Doctor speaks with straight tongue, Henry. Let's go."

Dr. Ross said, "I'll expect Mr. Lawson back by four o'clock, Captain, for his treatment."

"Four o'clock?" asked Sergeant Wheeler from the doorway.

"Sharp," said Dr. Ross.

Bubba and Johnny and Laura sat where they were and stared in apprehension as Captain Barnes crossed the room, took hold of Henry's arm and ushered him with determined gentleness to the door. Johnny said, "Jesus, Dr. Ross, is this okay? Shouldn't we have attorneys or something?"

Captain Barnes looked at Johnny from behind Henry's lowered head. "None of you are suspects. You were all here at the time of the explosion, right, locked up in your private rest home? So none of you is going to be charged with any kind of offense, and none of you will need an attorney. All you're doing is voluntarily helping the police department with its enquiries. You understand?"

"What's voluntary about it if we don't want to go?" said Johnny.

"I'll tell you what's voluntary about it," grated Captain Barnes. "If you don't come down to the precinct and answer my questions fully and freely, I'm going to make sure that this half-assed phobia setup is closed down tomorrow, and that all of you turkeys are sent back where you belong. On the farm."

"Captain," put in Dr. Ross coldly, his head held high and his eyes slitted. "Before you start making threats of that nature, just remember that any attempt to close this program has to go through all the proper judicial and medical channels."

Captain Barnes pushed Henry through the door, and Sergeant Wheeler led him through the main hall toward the office and the exit. "You remember something yourself, Doctor," said Captain Barnes as he left. "I can apply for a suspension of this program during my investigation if I feel that its continuance is an obstruction to myself or any of my officers. And, if I get that suspension, I can then make quite sure that neither you nor any of these loonies ever gets together again. Not for therapy, or discussion, or even an annual reunion of the homicidal maniacs club. You got me?"

"Get out of here," said Dr. Ross softly.

Captain Barnes closed the door. After he'd left,

Johnny got up and started pacing along the length of
the room, agitated and perspiring.

"Johnny," warned Dr. Ross.

"I can't help it," said Johnny. "This whole place feels
like it's closing in on me. Can't you open the door?
Can't you just please open the door?"

13

IT WAS LATER. The rain had eased off outside, and now a watercolor sun was shining on the hospital parking lot. Johnny, sedated, was sitting by the window of his room, staring out at the rows of cars. He was thinking about almost nothing at all, except some man who had once slept with his mother. A bearded man, quiet and careful in his movements. Somehow, Johnny had managed to escape from his cupboard and creep into his mother's bedroom. There had been a smell of cheap perfume and sex. His mother had been lying asleep, her hair tangled, her mouth slightly open, her legs drawn up like a child. The man had been standing naked in front of her dressing table, smoking a cigarette and thoughtfully watching himself in the mirror.

When Johnny had crept in, the man had said without smiling, "Hello, son," and Johnny had felt with an extraordinary rush of emotion and fear that at last he'd found his father. He had watched the man standing there smoking for almost ten minutes, and then the man had dressed himself in a dark blue sailor's uniform, left ten dollars on the dressing table and gone.

Not even a kiss for his own Johnny. Not even a wave from the street.

Further along the corridor Laura was lying on her

bed, reading a Regency romance called *Buck's Fire*. This was her own therapy, the treatment she had devised for herself. She tried to read the love scenes without feeling revolted by them, and to put herself in the place of the swooning heroines. All of these women *liked* having men push them to the ground and tear off their clothes, she thought. All of these women *liked* to be raped. *So what was wrong with me? Why did I hate it so much? Why did my rape make me so terrified of men that I can't even bear the way they look at me?*

She suddenly remembered the exact moment when she had picked up those long, pointed dressmaking scissors and chopped them into that man's face. She remembered his little clipped mustache, the color of his suit. She remembered how the first dark spurt of blood had splashed across her arm. She closed her eyelids and pressed her fingers against them to blot out the image. She had a curious fear that one day she might be tempted to poke out her own eyes, just to understand what that man had gone through.

The weak sunlight brightened up her room, and she shuddered.

Further along still, in the hall, both Bubba and Dr. Ross were sitting in The Box. The walls were blank, except for a pale back-projected glow, and the sound system was switched off completely to insulate them from the outside world.

Bubba was diffident, uncommunicative. His fingers were tapping on his knee. Dr. Ross was sitting straight, his arms folded, watching Bubba with complete confidence and complete control. On the floor beside him was a gabardine sack, tied at the neck with nylon string. Bubba had his eyes on the sack, and, even when Dr. Ross spoke to him, he wouldn't look away.

"Bubba," said Dr. Ross quietly.

Bubba didn't answer. He wiped his mouth with the back of his hand.

"Bubba," repeated Dr. Ross in the same even tone.

"I hear you," said Bubba.

"Okay, Bubba. I've told you what I'm going to do. I want you to be ready for it. I want you to be relaxed."

Bubba cleared his throat. "I'm relaxed," he said tightly. He was thinking of Barbara, and thinking of the way that Captain Barnes had taken Henry away that morning, and thinking most of all of his cell in the state penitentiary, with its view of an angled rooftop, and a chimney-stack, and nothing else at all.

Dr. Ross unfolded his arms, bent down and loosened the nylon string around the gabardine sack. Bubba let out a ridiculous, involuntary chuckle. *If he lets that thing out of there, I'm going to go crazy. I mean it. I'm going to go out of my mind. The very least I'm going to do is crap myself.*

"Okay, here we go," said Dr. Ross, and reached inside the bag. Something inside of the gabardine gave a stiff, swift wriggle. "I'm going to pick him up, okay? And I'm going to hold him in my hands, and then you can see for yourself that he won't hurt you. . . ."

"Dr. Ross—" said Bubba thickly.

Dr. Ross ignored him. He sat up straight in his chair again and raised his arms, and there, dangling between his hands, was a four-foot boa constrictor.

Bubba stared at the snake as if he'd seen the devil himself. "Oh, my sweet Lord," he said, and the words came out of his mouth like a child's building blocks collapsing. "I can't take this for one more moment, Dr. Ross. You have to take that thing away."

The snake curled itself around Dr. Ross's wrist and slowly began to slide up his arm. Bubba watched it in horrified fascination, rubbing at the back of his neck with his sweaty hand.

"I can't take it, Dr. Ross. I'm doing my best, I promise you. I'll really do good tomorrow. But please will you just please take that thing away right now?"

"Come on, Bubba, look at him." Dr. Ross grinned. "He's harmless. He won't hurt you. You could crush him with one hand if you wanted to. All you have to do is relax, and breathe deeply, and that's it."

Slowly Dr. Ross leaned forward again and set the boa down on the floor. It poured off his arm and began to make its way across the smooth white surface toward Bubba's chair. Bubba stared at it, his eyes popping with terror, his whole body locked rigid with the paralysis of utter fear.

"For Christ's sake, Dr. Ross, will you take it away? Will you just please take it away!"

Dr. Ross, still smiling, got up from his chair and picked the snake from the floor. But instead of returning it to the gabardine bag, he held it up in front of Bubba, only inches away from his face. The snake's tongue flickered as it tried to sense the vibrations in the air.

The heaviest vibration the snake was aware of was fear.

Bubba, with his eyes fixed immovably on the snake's flat head, said, "I'm going to get out of this chair, Dr. Ross, and I'm going to get myself over to that door, and I'm going to get out of here."

Dr. Ross shook his head. "You're staying, Bubba. You're staying and you're going to hold this snake."

"There ain't no way, Dr. Ross. I ain't kidding you none. There just ain't no way."

"You're not leaving, Bubba. You're going to stay here until this treatment is over. You remember what you promised to do for Barbara, don't you? You remember what you said this morning?"

"Listen, Dr. Ross, Barbara's dead now. She don't care what happens no more."

"She may not, Bubba. But I do. And I want you to hold this snake."

"Dr. Ross—"

"Look at him, Bubba! What has he done to you? Has he attacked you? Has he tried to strike you? This snake is as frightened of you as you are of him."

Dr. Ross held the snake only two inches away from Bubba's face. Bubba was grinning in fear, and his face was trickling with sweat.

"We've been working for months toward this," said Dr. Ross encouragingly. "Months, remember! All you have to do is touch him. That's all. Just touch him once, and I promise you that nothing will happen."

Bubba slowly raised his eyes toward Dr. Ross's face. There was no sympathy there. No weakness. Only that calm, even expression of complete determination which Bubba had come to admire so much and fear so deeply. Bubba trembled for a moment, and then took the kind of lung-scorching breath that sponge divers take before they dive into the ocean.

"That's it," said Dr. Ross soothingly as Bubba's right hand came up. "That's it, Bubba. He won't hurt you."

Bubba's hand quivered for a moment just an inch away from the snake's swaying head. Then he snapped his arm back against his side, and breathed, "I can't do it, Dr. Ross. There ain't no way."

"You want to go back to the pen, Bubba?" hissed Dr. Ross. "You want to spend the rest of your life shut up in that stinking cell?"

"No, sir. But I can't touch that snake."

"You're letting yourself down. You know that, don't you? You're proving to yourself that you're nothing but a coward and a washout."

"I can't touch that snake, Dr. Ross."

"Touch it, damn you! What do you think it's going to do to you? Swallow your big fat black carcass alive?"

"Dr. Ross!" said Bubba, agonized.

Keeping the snake aloft in his left hand, Dr. Ross reached down and took hold of Bubba's wrist. For a moment they were all leaning intimately together— Bubba, the snake and Dr. Ross. A strange tense triangle of three pairs of eyes, all differently involved in the same psychological crisis. Then Dr. Ross brought Bubba's arm up, as heavy and limp as the arm of a man asleep, and took it within a half-inch of the snake's tongue-flicking jaws.

"Dr. Ross," said Bubba. His voice was soft and resigned.

Dr. Ross held the snake and the arm like a man with two live electrical cables, poised to short circuit the world. Then he brought them together, snake and man, and Bubba shuddered and lolled back in his seat.

Dr. Ross waited for a while. Bubba sat with his head back, his eyes wide open and staring. He was breathing with his mouth open, harshly and slowly. Dr. Ross picked up the gabardine bag, dropped the snake back into it and tightened the drawstring.

"Bubba," he said, leaning over the West Indian and looking straight into his eyes. "Can you hear me, Bubba?"

"Yes, sir," Bubba answered. "I can hear you."

"Are you hurt, Bubba?"

"No, sir, I'm not."

"You touched the snake—do you realize that? You touched it and you got away with it."

"Yes, sir."

"You're doing fine, Bubba. You're making real progress. Next time, you can take the snake out of the bag yourself."

"Yes, sir."

Dr. Ross stood straight and paced across the white floor of The Box. Bubba stayed where he was, slumped in his chair, his breath gargling in his throat.

"You can, uh, you can go back to your room when you're ready," said Dr. Ross.

14

CAPTAIN BARNES INITIALED an incident report that was laid out on his desk in front of him, closed it and tossed it into his OUT basket. He stretched and yawned widely, and then he reached across to his intercom and pressed the button marked SGT. WHEELER.

"Sir?" answered Wheeler's voice, obviously with his mouth full.

"You can bring him in now," said Barnes. "That's if you've finished your doughnuts."

"Pizza, as a matter of fact, sir," replied Wheeler.

"I see," said Barnes. "Well, make sure you don't bring it into the office in the future. Not unless you bring me some too."

"Ten-four, sir."

Captain Barnes pushed back his chair and stood up. He was lucky to have a man like Roy Wheeler in his detective squad. Too many detectives these days were half-baked liberals who spent most of their time arguing about the social morality of chasing criminals, and who believed in what *Fortune* magazine called "the revolution of rising entitlements." Muggers were entitled to share in the national wealth by taking other people's purses, and murderers were entitled to the same kind of medical treatment and creature comforts as any other citizen.

But Roy Wheeler didn't think that way. Roy Wheeler, like Captain Barnes, was an officer of the old school. It wasn't that they didn't understand how poverty and prejudice and urban decay contributed to crime. They understood it better than most sociologists. They simply believed that, no matter how deprived a criminal was, he had no right to deprive anyone else of anything at all, whether it was jewelry, or credit cards, or life.

Behind their backs, Captain Barnes and Sergeant Wheeler were known as "the Archie Bunker Squad."

The door of Captain Barnes's office racketed open, and Henry Lawson was flung in so hard that he lost his balance and had to make a grab for the bookcase to stop himself from falling. Captain Barnes turned around in feigned surprise and stared at Henry the way a grade-school teacher stares at a small boy.

"What's the matter?" he demanded. "Are you drunk?"

Henry cleared his throat and adjusted his frayed tie. "No, sir. I guess I wasn't expecting the sergeant to push me, sir."

Sergeant Wheeler was standing in the doorway, grinning. Captain Barnes looked across at him expressionlessly, and then turned back to Henry.

"The sergeant's been treating you badly, huh?"

"No, sir. What I meant was that—"

"I'm not interested in what you meant," interrupted Captain Barnes. "This is a police precinct, not a rest home for the feeble-minded. Or perhaps that had escaped your notice?"

"No, sir, it hadn't," said Henry.

"Well, I didn't think it would"—Captain Barnes smiled—"considering the number of police precincts you must have seen in your time."

"What I meant was, sir, that—"

Captain Barnes slammed his open hand down on his desk. "Didn't you hear what I just told you? I don't care what you meant, or what you thought, or what you thought you meant, or anything. Do you understand me?"

"Yes."

"Maybe you still need a lesson in how to talk to a captain of detectives instead of a soft-headed psychiatrist?"

"No."

"What is this, Lawson? First you tell me 'yes,' then you tell me 'no.' Trying to give me a hard time, huh? Sit down!"

Captain Barnes gave Sergeant Wheeler the briefest of winks, and Sergeant Wheeler stepped quietly forward and took hold of the back of Henry's chair with both hands. Henry sensed that something was going on, and he turned around and frowned at Sergeant Wheeler suspiciously. Sergeant Wheeler kept on grinning like the Cheshire cat.

"Something wrong?" asked Captain Barnes.

"I don't know, sir," said Henry.

"You want Dr. Ross to come save your ass? Is that it? Look at me when I'm talking to you, do you understand?"

"Yes, sir."

"Okay, sit down," said Captain Barnes, and Henry, hesitantly, sat. Captain Barnes circled around his desk, then flipped open a sheet of crime reports with the back of his hand.

"Says here you used to work for the Gilbertville Quarry in Massachusetts."

"Yes, sir," said Henry, looking straight ahead of him. "It's all on my record."

"Reckon you know something about explosives then, working for a quarry?"

Henry nodded.

"Do you know something about explosives or don't you?" demanded Captain Barnes.

"A little," said Henry patiently.

"You could instruct someone how to plant a bomb? Tell them how to set the fuse, detonator, that kind of thing?"

"It isn't difficult."

"I didn't ask if it was difficult. I asked if you could do it."

Henry's eyelid twitched. "Yes, sir," he said. "I could do it."

"So you could have arranged for somebody to plant the bomb that killed Barbara Grey?"

"I could have done it, sir, except that I didn't."

Captain Barnes gave Henry a tight smile and walked up close to him. "You didn't, huh? Let me ask you something. You were with Cy Ferguson, weren't you, on that break-in job at Pepper Pike? Stripping the whole of the Hedley place while the unfortunate owners were away on vacation?"

Henry lowered his head. "Yes, sir, I was."

"But you were interrupted, weren't you, by two police officers who were alert enough and who had sufficient sense of duty to check the premises while the owners were away? And the rest of your miserable gang made it out of the back window onto the conservatory roof, didn't they? All except you, because it was eleven feet to jump and you were too damned scared. So you turned around with your gun and instead of jumping eleven feet you took the life of"——he checked the file ——"twenty-two-year-old Ernest Carter, a married man with a son of three and a daughter of eighteen months."

Henry was silent for a long time. Then he whispered, "Yes, sir."

Captain Barnes leaned over Henry, so close that Henry could feel the spit from his mouth when he emphasized a "t" a "d."

"You killed a man not because you were heroic," said Captain Barnes. "You killed a man because you were yellow. It says here you have a son, working for an electronics corporation in California."

"Yes, sir."

"Does your son know what you did? Or why?"

"I haven't heard from my son for years," said Henry tiredly. "I guess he disowned me a long time ago."

"And do you blame him?"

Henry took out his handkerchief and blew his nose.

"Do you blame him?" repeated Captain Barnes, more loudly.

"No, sir. I don't blame him."

Captain Barnes turned away from Henry again, and prowled around his desk some more, his hands thrust into his pants pockets. Sergeant Wheeler stayed where he was, still holding the back of Henry's chair. Outside, they could hear the whoop-whoop-whoop of a patrol car.

"*Now*," said Captain Barnes, "*now* you're all cozy at the Lakeshore. In the Titus E. Frobisher wing. The Disney Vacation World for homicidal fruitcakes."

"Sir, I—"

"What kind of a con did you use on that damned fool Ross to get in there, huh?" rapped Barnes. "Did you tell him what a respectable gent you were? What an upright, upstanding citizen? All a mistake, was it, when you blew twenty-two-year-old Ernest Carter inside out?"

"It wasn't a con," said Henry, in a shaky but defiant voice. "The warden told us they were looking for inmates with phobias, and I have this phobia about heights and falling."

"Well, you don't say," said Captain Barnes. "Stand up when I'm talking to you! Show some respect!"

Henry, with the obedience of a man who has spent twenty out of his fifty-odd years in institutions and prisons, stood up. Behind him, soundlessly, Sergeant Wheeler removed his chair.

"What are you standing for? *The Star-Spangled Banner?* Sit down!" barked Barnes.

Henry sat. At the split second when he realized the chair had gone, and that he was falling, his face was blank with terror. He hit the floor hard, banging his hip bone, and rolled over. Sergeant Wheeler smugly replaced the chair.

"What was that all about?" asked Captain Barnes. "When I tell you to sit down, I don't expect you to fall down. God Almighty! What are you trying to do? Give *me* a phobia?"

Henry climbed painfully to his feet and sat down again. Sergeant Wheeler couldn't hold back a snort of laughter.

"Wheeler," said Barnes slowly, "what do they call a guy who's too scared to admit he's a failure?"

"Chicken, I guess," grinned Wheeler.

Captain Barnes pointed at Henry as if he was identifying someone in court. "That isn't a chicken. If you called *that* a chicken, I reckon you'd be casting a slur on every poor creature that ever came out of Colonel Sanders' in a red and white striped tub. No, Wheeler, that is a fink. And not just your ordinary fink, either. That is a yellow fink. And because that is a yellow fink, that wants out of the phobia program."

Henry raised his head. "You're wrong there, Captain. I don't want out."

"Of course you don't want out. You like that nice cozy hospital."

"It's nothing to do with any nice cozy hospital. I'm there to get myself cured of my phobia."

"You expect me to believe that? Listen, fink, I've seen what you people have to do at that hospital. All you have to do is say that you're not scared of a few movies, and you're cured."

"You don't understand—" protested Henry.

"I understand all right!" snapped Captain Barnes. "I understand that yellow is yellow! Now, stand up, you yellow sonofabitch!"

Henry hesitated. Then he got slowly onto his feet. He stood looking at Captain Barnes with a fixed expression, making an effort to avoid the sullen stare which the warders classified as "dumb insolence," and beat you for.

"All right," said Barnes. "Now sit down."

Henry was afraid to sit, afraid to look behind to make sure the chair was there. He crouched slightly, putting his arms out below him, until his fingers clasped the edges of the seat. Then he sat down.

Captain Barnes smiled beatifically. "Did you see that, Wheeler?" he asked.

"Yes, sir," grinned Sergeant Wheeler. "I guess he doesn't trust me."

"Don't you trust the sergeant?" Captain Barnes demanded of Henry.

"Yes, of course," said Henry quickly.

"Then stand up!"

Henry stood up, cautious and frightened.

"Now sit down!" yelled Barnes. And as Sergeant Wheeler spun the chair away, Barnes gave Henry a push in the chest, so that Henry staggered, reached for a chair that wasn't there anymore and fell to the floor again, winded.

"Get up, you idle bastard!" roared Barnes. "You don't lie down in the middle of an interrogation!"

Henry climbed onto his feet, trembling. There was a red bruise on his left cheek, and he was breathing heavily.

"All right," Barnes whispered in a hoarse voice. "You sit down properly in your chair and you behave yourself. If you keep making my sergeant jump around like that, you're going to make him mad."

"I'll try," said Henry weakly.

"Okay." Captain Barnes smiled. "You were telling us you want to get out of the phobia program?"

"No, sir, I want to be cured."

Captain Barnes ignored him, as if he hadn't spoken at all. "You want to get out of the phobia program and you're too scared to admit that you can't be cured."

"Captain," said Henry, "I can't help myself. I'm afraid of heights and that's it."

"Oh, yes," sneered Barnes. "That's what they all say. 'Your Honor, I couldn't help it. I wasn't responsible for my actions.' I've heard enough of that bullshit to fertilize half of Iowa."

"Captain, I—"

"You don't have to explain," said Barnes. "We know what you did, and why you did it. The only reason we invited you along here was to have you sign your confession. You know what the fink did, Wheeler?"

"No, sir," said Wheeler, in a deliberately country-cousin voice. "What did he do?"

"He knew he was going to flunk the phobia program. He knew he wasn't getting any better. But he didn't want to go back to the slammer, did he? He didn't want that chance of early parole to slip out of his fingers.

So what did he think? He thought if he could get rid of Dr. Ross, who's the only guy who really knows how bad or how good those white rats are getting on, then he might still stand a chance of a break."

"This is insane!" said Henry.

"You're right," smiled Captain Barnes. "It *is* insane. But *you* did it, my friend. *You* were the one who arranged to have a heavy charge of plastic explosive planted on the side of Dr. Ross's filing cabinet. *You* were the one who couldn't face any more of those sessions in The Box. *You* were the one who thought the only way out was to blow Dr. Ross into small pieces. You killed a man once before because of your phobia, my friend, and now you've done it again."

"I can't believe what I'm hearing!" said Henry, standing up in horror. "How can you say that I'd try to kill Dr. Ross? He's the only damned friend I've got!"

Captain Barnes blinked at him. "I'm sorry?" he asked.

"I didn't do it!" insisted Henry. "I didn't have anything to do with it!"

"You didn't have anything to do with what?" asked Captain Barnes.

"With blowing up the doctor's apartment," said Henry, puzzled.

"Did I say you did?"

"Well, yes, you said that I was responsible. You said that I did it because I was flunking the phobia program."

Captain Barnes slowly shook his head. "I don't remember saying that. That doesn't sound like any kind of a motive to me. Did you hear me saying anything like that, Sergeant?"

Sergeant Wheeler shook his head too.

"For Christ's sake," said Henry. "You've just ac-

cused me of killing someone, and now you're trying to
pretend you didn't!"

"Are you calling me a liar?" barked Captain Barnes.
He shoved Henry hard in the chest, and, as Henry
grappled behind him for his chair, Sergeant Wheeler
swung it away again. Henry sprawled across the floor
and collided heavily with the side of the bookcase. He
got up onto his knees and crouched there, stunned.

"Well, now," said Captain Barnes, pacing with precise steps around his desk. "You said you weren't very
good when it came to falling, didn't you, Henry? But
I'd say you were pretty expert at it. You haven't done
anything but fall down since you came in here."

The captain returned to his desk and sat down, rest-
ing his chin on the palm of his right hand. He smiled
at Henry like a schoolmaster.

"What would Dr. Ross say if he could see you on
your knees? Jabbering and blabbering like an idiot
about standing and sitting and who knows what other
garbage? You don't have a phobia, Henry. You're just
plain nuts."

Henry didn't look up. He stayed where he was, his
shoulders hunched, his face turned away. Captain
Barnes nodded his head to Sergeant Wheeler, and the
sergeant crossed the room and laid a hand on Henry's
shoulder.

"Come on, fruitcake," said Sergeant Wheeler. "Up
on your feet."

Henry was well past fifty but he knew just what he
was going to do, and his speed took both of the detectives by surprise. He jerked up to his feet and
caught Sergeant Wheeler under the chin with the top
of his close-cropped head. The crack of bone against
bone was so loud that Captain Barnes thought a piece
of furniture had broken. Sergeant Wheeler said, *"erh!"*
and pitched backwards, stumbling over the chair.

Henry had wrenched open the door and was running along the corridor before Captain Barnes had even risen from his chair. Barnes tugged his gun from his shoulder holster, cannoned across to the doorway, and then pounced into the corridor in the classic legs-apart, two-hands-on-the-pistol shooting posture, something he hadn't done in a long time.

The corridor was empty. Henry had already gone. And then, as damned lousy luck would have it, that smooth-assed Lieutenant Parelli came out of his office and saw Captain Barnes standing there, bow-legged and ready to shoot, and gave him a calm, sarcastic smile.

"Keep the feet a little nearer together next time, Captain," he said. "But it's good to see that you practice whenever you can."

Sergeant Wheeler came to the door with his lip bleeding. "Where'd that mother go?" he growled.

"Lost someone?" asked Parelli.

"You mind your own goddamned business," snapped Captain Barnes, and thrust his short-barreled Python back in its holster. "Come on, Sergeant, let's get the hell out of here."

Lieutenant Parelli watched them go, a quirky smile on the corner of his mouth. A uniformed officer came along the corridor carrying a bundle of files, and Lieutenant Parelli stopped him.

"What's eating the Archie Bunker Squad?" he wanted to know.

The uniformed officer took out a mentholated inhaler and stuck it up his nose. "I think they just lost a murder suspect," he said in a cold voice. "Some old guy came beating it down the corridor like a bat out of hell and didn't stop for nobody."

"You mean that Captain Barnes lost a murder suspect out of his *office?* Right in the middle of *questioning?*"

"Looks that way, sir."

Lieutenant Parelli's lips tightened as he tried very hard not to laugh. "Good work, officer," he told the policeman, and went to find someone to tell.

15

HENRY CROSSED THE street in front of the police precinct and then he slowed down to a hurried walk. His head ached from butting Sergeant Wheeler, and his lungs felt as if they were full of blazing kerosene. Images jostled in front of his eyes—faces, people, taxis, buildings—and it wasn't until he had pushed his way along Clark Avenue to the corner of Fulton that he realized the significance of what he had done.

He hadn't only escaped from Captain Barnes and Sergeant Wheeler. He had escaped from custody altogether. For the first time in years, he was free.

He stopped in an office doorway, leaning against the stainless-steel paneling, trying to catch his breath. My God, if only he were ten years younger. He'd be so damned far away by now that they'd never catch him. A ride on Highway 2 to Toledo, and across the Canadian border before that crazy bastard Barnes could get a sniff of him. He looked at his misty, fingerprint-smeared reflection in the stainless-steel panel opposite, and he saw a gray, thin ghost. Henry Lawson, he thought. The hopeful boy, the nervous student, the confused and unsuccessful man. Why had he shot that poor young boy at Pepper Pike? Why hadn't he thrown

126

away his gun and put up his hands and taken five years for burglary? Even five years was better than dying.

Rested, but still breathing heavily, he left the doorway and made his way across the street. He didn't quite know where he was going, but he trotted on with doggedness and determination, and it wasn't until he was close to the new condominium complex at Lorain Avenue that he saw the dark green Pontiac Bonneville turning the corner behind him and realized that Captain Barnes wasn't going to let him go. He started to run harder, along the side of a new building site, past fences and hoardings and site huts, and he prayed with every breath that he would get away.

Henry knew, knew, knew that he wasn't responding to the phobia treatment. Not as well as Dr. Ross expected him to, anyway. But what did Dr. Ross want? Miracles? Henry was terrified of heights and it was going to take more than a few high-altitude movies to cure him. They were stunning and frightening, those movies in The Box. They were almost as frightening as the real thing. But Henry had been looking for more than endless simulations of the fear he already knew. Henry had been looking for *guidance*, for an explanation of his phobia, and how to overcome it. That was where Dr. Ross had failed him. Dr. Ross had never made him feel as if his phobia was anything but wrong. It's *wrong* to be afraid, it's *right* to be brave.

And somehow, although he respected Dr. Ross, and counted him as a friend, Henry felt that The Box treatment was nothing more than the human equivalent to the old technique of rubbing a puppy's nose in its own mess.

He wished to God that Dr. Ross was with him now.

He glanced over his shoulder, and the Pontiac was closer. He tried to run faster, and it was then that the siren suddenly started up, piercing and weird. They must have seen him. It was only a matter of time and they'd catch him. He turned quickly into the gates of the construction site, and hurried down the ramp that led to the side of the building.

He didn't look up. Heights were just as dizzying from the ground as they were from the top. Above him, still mostly in steel framework, rose the twenty-five-story Euclid Insurance Building, crisscrossed and rusty against a gray sky, and, next to it, a tower crane that was slowly swinging buckets of reinforced concrete materials across to the men working ten floors up. There was a constant bellowing of diesel engines, and an ear-splitting chorus of rivet guns and hammers.

Henry stepped gingerly over planks and pipes and muddy ruts. At the corner of the building farthest away from the gates, he turned and looked back to see if Captain Barnes was following him. He couldn't run anymore; he was too exhausted, and he didn't know if he was feeling cold or hot. But the dark green Bonneville was just turning into the entrance and bouncing slowly down the muddy ramp.

Taking a deep breath, he made his way along the back of the building. He was only halfway along, panting and tired, when he heard someone shout, "Hey, buddy! Hey, you!"

He pretended he hadn't heard, and tried to keep going, but the voice repeated, "Hey, you! I'm talking to you!"

He turned. A fat-bellied foreman in a smeary white hard hat and a checkered shirt was trudging purposefully toward him, his boots thick with mud.

"You from Prosser's?" demanded the foreman.

"Prosser's?"

"The architects. Well, if you don't know them, I guess you're not. You should be wearing a hard hat."

"I, er, I was just taking a look, that's all."

"I'm sorry, buddy, this site is strictly for permitted personnel only. I'm going to have to ask you to leave."

Henry gave him an uneasy smile. "Oh? Permitted personnel only? In that case—well, in that case, I'll go. Sorry."

"Just beat it before anyone else sees you."

Henry turned the corner and there, at the far end of the site, stood Captain Barnes and Sergeant Wheeler. They both had their guns out, and they were looking around the site like weekend husbands looking for their wives in a shopping crowd.

Henry looked up. Halfway along the building, in between him and Captain Barnes, rose a temporary elevator cage. It was just descending now, cluttered with bent fragments of reinforcing rods and rubbish from the tenth story. It reached ground level with a bang, and two workmen started to empty it.

Henry, watched from behind by the foreman, started to walk along the side of the building. From the opposite end, Captain Barnes started walking toward him. Barnes hadn't seen him yet, but it was only going to be a matter of seconds before he did. Henry lowered his head, so that Barnes wouldn't recognize him so quickly, and plodded through the mud and the rubble as fast as he could.

The workmen had finished clearing the elevator now. They pulled off the last length of rusty steel rod, and pressed the button for the men on the tenth floor to take the cage up again. Henry heard the buzz of the starter signal, and he knew that this was his last possible chance. He put his head up and started to run.

"*Wheeler!*" yelled Barnes. "*He's here!*"

Henry ran as fast as his middle-aged legs could take him. One of the workmen who had been clearing the elevator started to move toward him, his face set in a frown, but Henry pushed the man aside with the best

block he'd done since college, and scrambled into the
rising elevator cage before anyone else could stop him.
He scraped his knee badly and bruised his elbow, but
the elevator took him up and away before Barnes could
get anywhere near him.

He thought he saw Barnes raising his gun. But the elevator was passing through a whole pattern of girders and
uprights, and the dangers of a ricochet were too great.
He rose past the fourth, fifth, sixth and seventh stories,
still kneeling on the gritty floor of the cage, and suddenly Captain Barnes and Sergeant Wheeler and all the
rest of the construction site began to look terrifyingly
small.

He knelt up, with his back straight, and closed his
eyes. He hoped to God he was going to be able to hold
onto his sanity. The ground was already too far away
for him to look at, and all he could see was sky, and
the tops of the buildings of downtown Cleveland, and
even beyond, to the lake. Tiny cars were beetling along
Clifton Avenue, and a police helicopter appeared to
be flying below him. The gray afternoon light fell in
flickering lozenge shapes on his face as he rose up and
up between the girders. There was no sound but the
wind and the clattering of the elevator.

Captain Barnes watched the cage rise past the tenth
floor and keep on going upward.

"Can't you stop that damned thing?" he asked the
foreman.

"I could cut the power, I guess," the foreman said.
"But I'd have to ask the site manager first."

"That's a homicide suspect in there!" rasped Barnes.
"Just cut the damned power and ask the site manager
afterward!"

The elevator rose past the eighteenth floor and kept
on going.

"Don't reckon there's a lot of point," said the foreman. "By the time we could shut down the generator, the cage would be right at the top."

"Jesus Christ!" breathed Barnes in exasperation.

Inside the elevator cage, Henry had managed to pull himself up onto his feet, clinging to one of the uprights. He kept his eyes on the wire fencing around the cage, and made a deliberate effort not to focus on the distant view of the city of Cleveland beyond it. His brain felt as if it was tilting, and his insides had turned to cold water. It's just a movie, he tried to tell himself. Just another of Dr. Ross's back-projections. I'm not really here at all.

But then the elevator clattered to a stop on the twenty-fifth floor. Up here, there was no concrete. Just a lattice of steel girders, open to the sky. Three construction workers in plaid shirts and hard hats were sitting with their lunchpails and their flasks of coffee, perched on the edge of the building as casually as if they were sitting on a park bench downtown.

The wind blew noisily in Henry's ears and fluttered the tails of his coat. He stood in the elevator cage, his sweaty hands tight on the rusty steel upright, and he was too frightened even to pray. Far below him, he could see Brookside Park, and the waterfront, and the American League Ball Park. Off to the west, glistening in the hazy daylight, airplanes were landing and taking off from Hopkins International Airport.

"Oh, my God," he whispered. "Oh, my God, protect me."

The three construction workers had seen him now, and one of them had put down his lunch pail on a narrow steel beam, and was balancing over toward him.

"Hey, fella!" he called. "You sure you're supposed to be up here?"

"Where's your safeties?" yelled out one of his workmates.

Henry retreated back across the cage, grabbing the upright on the opposite side. Below him, he glimpsed the elevator shaft, dropping twenty-five stories to the ground, and for a split second he saw the tiny pink grublike figures of Captain Barnes and all the other construction workers who were looking up at him. A black and white police car was driving onto the building site with its red lights flashing and its siren moaning, and the police helicopter had banked and turned over Fairview Park and was making its way back.

"Come on, now, fella," said the construction worker, as he reached the elevator. "All you have to do is reverse the switch, and the elevator will take you straight back down again."

Henry didn't look at him. "Just keey away," he said, his throat tight with fear.

"Listen," said the construction worker. "I'm just going to help you get back down again, that's all."

"I'll jump!" said Henry.

"No, no, you wouldn't do a thing like that," said the construction worker, balancing closer still.

Henry took one hand away from the upright, and the construction worker froze.

"Fella," he said, "that's all of four hundred feet to the ground there. They'll still be picking you up next Thanksgiving."

Henry tentatively stepped from the elevator cage to the steel girder on the opposite side from where the construction worker was standing. Biting his lip in tension, he reached out for a handhold, and gradually edged his way out of the elevator and along the girder to a vertical H-beam.

"Listen, buddy, you just hold on tight there, and don't let go," said the construction worker.

Henry inched his way along further. He couldn't reach the next vertical beam without balancing along the foot-wide girder unsupported, and for a moment he hesitated and swayed. But then, like a somnambulist, he shuffled the two or three feet along the girder to the next upright, and clung on. The construction worker wiped sweat from his forehead with his sleeve.

"I want Dr. Ross, that's all," said Henry. "Just tell them to go get Dr. Ross."

"Who?" asked the construction worker.

"Dr. Ross!" called Henry, hoarsely. "I won't come down for anyone else!"

The construction worker took out a chewed ballpen and a grubby piece of paper. "What's his number?" he asked Henry. "Tell me his number and I'll have the foreman call him. And for Christ's sake, don't look down!"

"I want Dr. Ross!" Henry screeched.

"Okay, okay," said the construction worker. "You just hang on in there, will you?"

The construction worker's two buddies had walked along to the elevator now, and were watching Henry anxiously.

"What does he want?" one of them asked.

"Some doctor. Says he'll jump if we don't get him."

"Okay. We'll stay here. You go down and see what the hell's going on."

The construction worker clambered into the elevator cage, pulled the switch, and the elevator sank toward the ground. Henry, holding tight onto his upright beam, felt the vibration of its winding gear as it went down. In the distance he could see Shaker Heights, and the very idea of being able to see so far made him feel paralyzed with terror. Don't look down, the man had said. He clung on to the H-beam as if it was his own mother, and he pressed his forehead against the rusty steel.

It seemed to take hours for the elevator to reappear. The first he knew of it was the rattling in the steel beams. Then the cage rose into view, and there was the construction worker again, with Captain Barnes, the foreman, and Sergeant Wheeler.

"Guy's crazy," he heard the construction worker saying. Then Barnes stepped out of the cage, holding onto his hat to stop the wind from blowing it away, with Wheeler just behind him.

"Lawson!" shouted Barnes. *"You get back here!"*

Henry shook his head.

"If you don't get back here by the time I count to three, I'm going to put your ass back in the slammer for the rest of your natural-born days!" yelled Barnes. *"Now, turn around, and start walking!"*

Barnes took a step along the girder, but Henry raised one hand, and screamed, "If you come any closer, you bastard, I'll jump!"

The construction worker held Captain Barnes's sleeve. "Seems to me he's serious, buddy. And he could take you down with him."

Captain Barnes looked narrowly at the construction worker, his eyes watering in the wind, and then he looked down toward the ground. He could see police cars arriving, a paramedic ambulance and clusters of people. It was a hell of a long way down.

"Henry," said Captain Barnes, more evenly. "I want you to make your way back to the elevator. Do you understand me? Make your way back, one step at a time, and don't look down."

"I want Dr. Ross!" shouted Henry.

"Henry, I'm not going to hurt you!" insisted Captain Barnes. "Everything that happened in my office—well, that was all a misunderstanding! You just come back here and we'll talk it over!"

Captain Barnes took a step nearer, but Henry let go of the vertical H-beam and began to teeter on the edge of the girder.

"You get back!" shrilled Henry. "You get back, or I'll jump!"

Captain Barnes quickly retreated. "Get Ross," he told Sergeant Wheeler. "I don't care where he is. Get on that goddamned bleeper and get him up here."

"But Captain, he could be anywhere."

Captain Barnes glared at Wheeler fiercely. "Will you just do as you're damn well told, and get him?"

"Yes, sir. Right away, sir."

Wheeler went back to the elevator, where he'd left his two-way radio. He picked it up and began to talk into it, quickly and emphatically. Captain Barnes stayed where he was, the high wind rippling his raincoat, watching the poor creature who was huddling in his gray suit on a narrow girder on the twenty-fifth floor, his face white with cold, his hands tightly gripping the rusted six-inch beam which was all that was separating him from the realization of his most terrible nightmares.

16

DR. ROSS WAS jogging in the gardens opposite his house. He was running with the slow, easy, controlled strides of a practiced athlete, boxing at shadows as he ran under the trees. A few feet behind him, Jenny was doing her best to keep up. If you'd seen them from a distance—Dr. Ross in his dark blue professional warm-up suit and Jenny in her white pullover and her ski hat—you wouldn't have guessed that they were even jogging together. It was only when they turned the corner of the pathway opposite Dr. Ross's apartment house on Argyle Street that Jenny suddenly called out to Dr. Ross, and he hesitated, and slowed, and came backpedaling to see what the matter was.

"Can't we take a breather?" she said. "I'm p-double-oh-p-e-d."

"Huh?" he frowned, dancing lightly all around her in his running shoes.

"Pooped," she explained.

"We haven't even started," he told her. "This is just to get the circulation going. Didn't anyone ever tell you it was harmful to jog with a cold body?"

"Sure. They told me it was harmful to jog with an exhausted body, too."

"We have a mile to go," he said, "at least."

"Why should I jog another mile? I can get fit just watching you dancing around like Muhammed Ali. You take it pretty seriously, don't you?"

Dr. Ross let off a flurry of punches against the wind. "You want me to lose my place on the team? 'Dr. Peter Ross . . . oh, yeah, I remember him . . . gave up jogging and went all to flab . . . Ross the Rotund, we call him. . . .' "

"Not you. You're too competitive. Do you do this every day?"

"Sure. Sometimes I jog to the hospital."

"Whew, I think you're crazy."

They started off again, a very slow jog now, scarcely running at all. They passed the main entrance and turned toward a path that would lead them under an avenue of oaks.

"This is where Barbara was walking only yesterday, wasn't it?" said Jenny. "Through this park and out into the street over there?"

"That's right," said Ross, quickening his pace a little.

"Doesn't it make you feel—I don't know—kind of regretful?"

"Why should it?"

Jenny fell back a few inches, frowning. Dr. Ross was going like a well-coordinated machine now, his shoes padding almost silently on the Tarmac path.

"Why *should* it? Well—it just should!"

Dr. Ross put on one final burst of speed, and then slowed down to a walk again. "Yes, I guess you're right. She was a good patient. Really promising."

Jenny took his arm. "Is that going to be her epitaph? 'She was a really promising patient'?"

"What do you want me to do, go into mourning for a week?"

"I don't know. I guess I just want to see some kind of response. I mean, supposing it had been me?"

He shrugged and let out a long breath of resignation. "If I felt emotional about those people, Jenny, I'd be torn to shreds by now. They're weak, they're disadvantaged, they're crammed up to their eyeballs with irrational fears. I'm trying to cure them, as a scientist, and the only way I can be any use to them is if I keep hold of my scientific objectivity."

"Objectivity sounds so callous," she said.

He started jogging again. "It's all there is. For those people, anyway."

Jenny ran faster, trying to keep pace. "I've hurt your feelings, haven't I?" she said. "I didn't mean to. Please, Peter, forgive me."

He stopped running, beside a tree. The wind was rustling so noisily through the leaves that she could scarcely hear what he was saying. But the way he held her hands, and the way he looked into her eyes—neither of those left her in any doubt at all.

"Listen, Jenny," he said. "I love you. I never knew I could care for anyone the way I care for you. There's never going to be anyone like you ever."

He said something else, but she couldn't quite catch it. But then he leaned forward and kissed her, slowly, with the warmth and relish of a real lover.

"Oh, Peter," she whispered, hugging him tight.

Something went *blip-blip-blip-blip*.

"What's that?" she said, startled.

He reached down and unclipped his bleeper from his belt. Without answering her, he switched it off and said, "I have to get to the phone."

"The hospital?"

"Probably. I told them not to bother me unless it was an emergency."

He turned and began to run back the way they'd come. Jenny started after him, but by the time she'd reached the main entrance, he was out of sight. It was only when she came panting along the sidewalk outside the park that she saw him standing by the open door of his Porsche, talking on the phone. She covered the last few feet as quickly as she could, but by the time she got there he was tugging a pair of trousers on over his jogging pants. He shrugged on his tweed coat, pulled the collar straight, and shouted, "It's Henry! Get in the car, quick!"

"What's the matter?" she asked breathlessly.

"I'll tell you later! Just get in the car!"

Jenny climbed in and buckled up her seat belt. Dr. Ross slid in next to her, switched on the engine and slammed the Porsche into second. The sports car took off from the curb with a skittering howl of tires and a cloud of blue smoke. Dr. Ross U-turned, almost colliding with a truck, and sped south through the mid-afternoon traffic toward Euclid Avenue.

"Henry's all right, isn't he?" asked Jenny, her face pale. "I mean, he's not—?"

"Not yet," said Dr. Ross tersely. "But he could be, by the time we get there."

17

HENRY, FROM THE ground, looked no more significant than a stray bird. A small dark figure perched on the very corner of the building's steel framework, his hair disheveled and his coat flapping in the wind. He had edged further along since Captain Barnes had ordered Sergeant Wheeler to put out the call for Dr. Ross, and now it was impossible for anyone to reach him from the elevator platform without giving him plenty of time to make up his mind to jump.

The police had cleared the site below the building to a distance of one hundred and fifty feet. That, based on practical experience, was how far the suicide squad anticipated that pieces of Henry would probably be scattered. Should he actually jump, of course, or fall. Several jumpers, having decided against suicide after all, had lost their footing through fear or tiredness, and had taken their last dive involuntarily.

Dr. Ross drove his Porsche down the building-site ramp and across the muddy unloading area where all the police cars and ambulances were parked. Captain Barnes saw him coming, and walked stiffly across to meet him, with Sergeant Wheeler only a short way behind.

"Thanks for coming so quick," said Barnes, peering

in at the car window. "He says you're the only person he wants to talk to."

"What happened?" asked Dr. Ross. "How the hell did he get up there?"

Captain Barnes didn't answer, but continued to stare through the Porsche's window as if he was arresting Dr. Ross for a traffic violation. Sergeant Wheeler said, "The guy's nuts. No two ways about it."

Dr. Ross climbed out of his car and slammed the door. Jenny stayed where she was for a moment, and then climbed out too, more cautiously.

An officer from the Cleveland fire department was standing close by, talking to reporters. Dr. Ross walked across to him, took his arm, and said, "Isn't there any way to save him? A net, or something?"

The fireman glanced at Captain Barnes quizzically, but Barnes nodded to tell him that it was okay to speak.

"A net isn't usually worth trying over four stories," the fireman explained. "At this height, twenty-five stories, we might just as well try to catch him in a wet Kleenex."

Dr. Ross shaded his eyes against the gray brightness of the day. "In that case," he said, "Ive got to get up there."

The construction foreman said, "Sorry, Doctor. It aint worth it."

"Why not?"

"He's frozen to that beam now. Even if you talked him into coming in, he couldn't make it. The gusts are getting up. No."

"How did he get up there?" asked Dr. Ross. "Surely he could be coaxed back the same way?"

"I've seen it before," said the foreman. "They're in a real frenzy when they go out there, but after they've sat on their butts in a high wind for an hour, they've lost all their nerve. He'd only have to look down once, and you'd have lost him."

"So what do we do?" demanded Dr. Ross. "Wait until he drops off through sheer exhaustion? That's a man up there. A human being."

"A homicidal maniac, to boot," said Captain Barnes, loud enough for Dr. Ross to hear, but not for anyone else.

The construction foreman turned his head around, and looked up at the tower crane.

"Listen," he said, "if you're really set on getting up there . . . maybe the crane could lift you. We could put you in the bucket . . . hoist you up to the twenty-fifth . . . then maybe you could get him to swing himself inside."

Captain Barnes said, "That's ridiculous. He'd take one look at the bucket coming toward him and jump."

"Not if he knew it was me," retorted Dr. Ross. "And what difference does it make to you, anyway? You want him to jump, don't you? One less crazy killer to worry about?"

Sergeant Wheeler moved forward threateningly, but Captain Barnes raised his arm and held him back.

"All right, Doctor. You want to play Batman. Get up there and do your stuff."

Already the construction foreman had contacted the crane operator on his walkie-talkie, and the massive boom of the crane was angling across the building site. The men watched as the huge concrete-encrusted bucket was lowered on its cables, and hit the ground with a heavy crunch.

"That bucket's too deep for a man to stand in," said the foreman. "Get some of those boxes they packed the floor tiles in, and see if you can fill her up halfway."

Dr. Ross and Captain Barnes waited impatiently while the workmen went off to find boxes and rubbish to

fill up the bucket. Jenny stood behind them, not wanting
to interfere, but she couldn't stop herself from looking
up to the top of the building from time to time, and
staring at the forlorn figure of Henry Lawson. Sergeant
Wheeler sidled up to her and said, "Long drop, huh,
for a guy without a parachute?"

Jenny gave him a disdainful look and stepped two
or three paces away. Sergeant Wheeler blew his nose
loudly and grinned.

Eventually, after ten minutes, the construction foreman came plodding across to Dr. Ross with the news
that the bucket was stacked up enough for him to stand
in.

"I have to tell you that you're doing this at your own
risk," he said. "The only fun part of falling twenty-five
stories is the first twenty-four-and-a-half stories. After
that, it gets kind of dangerous."

"He's my patient," said Dr. Ross. "Let's get on with
it."

He turned, and Jenny was standing there, her face
white and anxious. She didn't move, didn't wave. All
she did was mouth the words "I love you." Dr. Ross
nodded, without smiling, and then he let the workmen
lead him across to the box-filled bucket.

The bucket's hinged side had been let down, so Dr.
Ross could walk up the sloping side, and then scramble
up the heap of boxes. The foreman whistled to the
crane operator, cables whirred and the hinged side was
slowly raised into position. Dr. Ross was left standing
in the bucket chest-high, holding on to the concrete-
encrusted sides for support.

"Are you ready?" the foreman asked him. Dr. Ross
gave a wave and nodded.

The cables tightened and then, quite suddenly, the
bucket was plucked up from the ground and began to
rise. Dr. Ross, balanced uncomfortably on a stack of

cardboard boxes and broken timber, saw the ground drop away from him. The bucket swung disconcertingly from side to side, and around and around, and as he was lifted upward the framework of the Euclid Insurance Building loomed alarmingly near and then tilted away again.

He passed the last of the concrete-clad floors, the tenth. A group of workmen were standing watching him as he rose past them. They neither called nor waved. Just watched. He looked up toward the twenty-fifth floor, and for a moment he saw Henry. Then the bucket spun around again, and the city of Cleveland revolved all around him.

The bucket was lifted past floor after skeletal floor. As it rose, it steadied, and by the time Dr. Ross reached the top of the building only the wind was making it sway. He waved to the crane operator that he wanted to be taken nearer to Henry's corner.

Henry was straddling the corner beams of the building, his eyes closed tight. His nose had been bleeding from the cold, and his hands were white. As Dr. Ross was brought in closer to him, he seemed to bow down, so that his forehead was almost touching the steel beam, but he still didn't open his eyes.

"Henry!" shouted Dr. Ross, against the wind. "Henry!"

Henry looked at him. The crane operator brought Dr. Ross a few feet closer, and Dr. Ross stretched his arms out in an attempt to catch the beam that Henry was sitting on, and steady the bucket. He missed only by inches.

"I want you to stand up, Henry—reach out and take my hands—" yelled Dr. Ross. "I won't let you fall—I promise you—"

The crane operator tried to nudge the bucket closer still. It dipped and swayed, and Dr. Ross, reaching over the side, almost lost his balance. For a second he saw the ground below him, and the police cars the size of miniature toys, and a surge of vertigo went through him like an electric shock.

Henry was kneeling on the beam now and shouting something. Dr. Ross could hear the words *"Barnes"* and *"chair"*, but the wind swallowed everything else.

Dr. Ross screamed, *"Stand up, Henry—stand up—then reach out and take my hands—"*

Henry stayed on all fours on the beam, an incongruous cat stuck up an insanely high tree. Then, slowly, he managed to climb to his feet, clawing at the wind as if it could support him.

On the ground below, through binoculars and telephoto lenses, they could see that Dr. Ross was shouting at Henry, encouraging him. They could see Henry reaching out, reaching out, and they could see Dr. Ross's hands outstretched. There could only have been two or three inches between their fingertips. The bucket swung and turned.

Then, there was silence. Henry was falling, and nobody spoke. He fell past the twentieth floor, the fifteenth, the tenth, and they couldn't do anything at all but watch him as he floated down out of the sky with his arms out wide and his head tilted toward the ground.

He seemed to take so long. Jenny watched him and had time to remember the foreman's black joke about the first twenty-four-and-a-half stories being fun. Then, Henry suddenly seemed to speed up, and there was a sound like a sack of Idaho potatoes being thrown into a heap of gravel.

Jenny heard the foreman snap into his intercom, "Get that bucket down, quick!" and at that moment everybody was running toward the place where Henry had fallen.

She hadn't ever in her whole life seen anything like it. In movies, people fell from buildings and lay there intact, still in their evening clothes, with a trickle of blood crossing the sidewalk, and only their *boutonniere* seeming to be crushed. Henry had burst apart, as if someone had pumped him up ten times his normal size with an air pump, and then stuck a pin in him. There was blood everywhere, and strings of gory things that Jenny couldn't even identify. She turned around as quickly as she'd run there, and stumbled away in no direction at all, feeling lightheaded and shocked.

She thought she heard Sergeant Wheeler saying, "Are you okay?" in a fuzzy sort of a voice, and then her salad lunch came gushing out of her mouth and there wasn't anything she could do to stop it.

18

THE EARLY-MORNING sunlight filled the studio so brightly that she seemed to be illuminated by her own halo. She was sitting at her easel as Dr. Ross walked through from the bedroom, making sketches in charcoal for her new sculpture. The faint *skritch-skritch* of her black charcoal twig was the only sound in the whole apartment.

"There's coffee on the stove," she told him.

He went over to the kitchen counter, buttoning up his shirt. A copy of the morning paper was lying there, neatly folded. He picked it up without a word and shook it out.

The headline read, CRIMINAL PSYCHO DIES IN 25-STORY PLUNGE.

"Have you seen this?" asked Dr. Ross.

Jenny nodded.

" 'Criminal psycho,' " he said bitterly. "The poor guy was terrified of heights, that's all."

He sat down at the butcher-block table, staring at the front-page photograph of himself, suspended in the bucket, blurrily reaching for Henry's outstretched arms. Down the side of the page was a series of small high-speed pictures of Henry falling.

Jenny laid down her charcoal, walked into the

kitchen and poured him a cup of coffee. She set it down in front of him, and he said, "Thanks."

"Don't you think that picture's beautiful?" asked Jenny.

"Beautiful?" asked Dr. Ross, and there was a touch of hostility in his voice.

"What I mean is, you were trying to save his life. Your hand reaching for his."

Dr. Ross slowly folded the paper up again and laid it down on the table. His face was impassive, except for a small muscle working in his right cheek. His front teeth were slightly crooked, and when he was tense he had a habit of grinding them together.

"Darling, you did everything you could," said Jenny softly. "It was just a terrible accident, that's all."

Dr. Ross stood up and walked across to the studio window. The light was so bright there that Jenny could hardly look at him. It dissolved his outline until he looked like one of the *Star Trek* crew members, just about to beam himself into infinity.

"He was almost there, you know that?" said Dr. Ross. "He went up that building alone. Alone! Can you understand what that means? The therapy was working. Two or three more sessions and I could have cured him."

Jenny looked away. "You can't blame yourself for it, Peter. It wasn't your fault."

He shook his head. "I'm not blaming myself. If I blamed myself, I wouldn't have been able to get out of bed this morning. I wouldn't be able to function. But I can function, because I must. I have three other patients to think about. Three other patients who need me."

He came away from the window. "I'm on the edge of breaking this thing, Jenny. In two, three weeks, I'm going to be the best-known psychological behaviorist in the whole damned country."

"Peter," she said gently.

He sipped his coffee. She came up close to him and held his sleeve.

"Peter," she said, "let's go away for a while."

"Away?" he asked. "What do you mean?"

"A vacation. A long weekend. Maybe a week. Just to forget some of this tragedy. . . ."

He shook his head. "I can't, Jenny. Not now. If I go away now, there won't be any program to come back to. Clegg's under pressure from the police and the prison service. Clemens is only happy as long as I keep flattering her. And as for that bastard Barnes . . . no, they'd shut me down the moment I turned my back."

"What about Dr. Alice Toland?"

"Alice? Well, she used to support what I was doing. But sometimes I think she'd like to see the phobia program shut down as much as the rest of them. I can't go away, honey. Not until the rest of the treatment is completed."

"It seems like you don't have any supporters left at all," said Jenny.

Dr. Ross turned to Jenny, set down his coffee cup and smiled at her. "I have you," he said quietly. He kissed her.

The brass sea clock on the wall chimed ten. Dr. Ross checked his watch and said, "Look at the time. I have to get out of here."

"Will you be back for supper?" she asked him.

He buttoned up his coat. "Depends what it is."

"Hungry Man TV dinner, turkey variety?"

"That'll do. Take care. I'll see you later."

He kissed her again, rushed halfway across the studio, came back, kissed her yet again and left. As the door banged behind him, she leaned against the table and smiled. He was something else, that Dr. Peter Ross. A bundle of energy, seriousness, conscientiousness, fun and dedication. A man who always had to swim up-river, against the current.

Outside in the hallway, Dr. Ross punched the elevator button. The elevator had been repaired, after a fashion, and it rumbled and creaked upward in a tardy response to his command. He rattled back the lattice gates, closed them behind him and pressed the button for the first floor. The elevator shook its way downward with all the infirmity of an old servant carrying a tray of sherry.

It would be jammed again by this evening, thought Dr. Ross, as he slid back the gates and stepped out. Might as well take advantage of it while it's still shaking along. . . .

19

CAPTAIN BARNES WAS waiting for him in his office. Sitting in Dr. Ross's chair, still wearing his raincoat, and swinging slowly backward and forward like a man with all the time in the world.

"Good morning," said Captain Barnes.

Dr. Ross picked up his mail, shuffled through it and then dropped it back on his desk again.

"Oh, yes?" he asked. "What's good about it?"

"You're still alive and kicking, for one thing," Captain Barnes remarked, standing up. "So whoever's been trying to knock you off hasn't succeeded yet. That's if he's still alive."

"What are you trying to suggest?"

"I'm not trying to suggest anything. I'm just trying to cover all the possibilities."

"You mean you believe that Henry could have been responsible for planting the bomb?"

Captain Barnes looked at Dr. Ross steadily. "He knew about explosives," he said. "What's more, he was desperately afraid of flunking the phobia course."

"That's ridiculous. They're *all* afraid of flunking it. That's what makes them work so hard at getting rid of their fears. Henry didn't have any more reason to kill me than any of the others."

"Or any less." Captain Barnes smiled.

Dr. Ross took off his coat, hung it over the back of his chair and then walked through into the old lecture hall, where The Box stood. Captain Barnes followed him, with his hands deep in his raincoat pockets.

"That's quite a structure you've got yourself there," said Barnes, peering into The Box's open door. "Maybe I could borrow it sometime, for an interrogation room."

He stepped inside. Dr. Ross reached over to the control panel and flicked the switch which closed the door. Then he switched on the intercom and the closed-circuit television monitor. He could see Barnes standing in The Box, placidly looking around him.

"What are *you* afraid of, Captain?" asked Dr. Ross over the intercom. "Most people have some kind of psychological wrinkle. Want me to iron it out for you?"

Captain Barnes turned around, to see where the voice was coming from. Then he said, "Only one thing gets me going, Dr. Ross. And that's people who lie."

Dr. Ross flicked two more switches. Immediately, the floor of The Box appeared to fall away under Captain Barnes's feet, and he was plummeting downward through bottomless space. Dr. Ross smiled as the detective crouched forward in nervous reaction to the back-projected illusion. Then he reached over and flicked another switch, and the walls of The Box became thundering waterfalls.

"Quite a trick," shouted Captain Barnes over the noise of the water. "Pity you're wasting it on those low-life killers."

Instantly, expressionlessly, Dr. Ross switched everything off and opened The Box's door. Captain Barnes waited for a moment, to see if anything else was going to happen, and then he stepped out.

"Usually," he said, walking slowly across to the electronic console, "usually we make a homicide arrest within the first twenty-four hours."

"Seems like you've run over your deadline," said Dr. Ross.

"Maybe. But we have a unique situation here. We're looking for a psychopathic killer among a whole bunch of psychopathic killers. We're searching for hay in a haystack, if you see what I mean. So the real killer isn't so easy to spot."

He circled the console and picked up a cassette tape. "Tapes of your treatment sessions?" he asked.

Dr. Ross nodded.

"I'd like to hear them."

"That isn't possible. They're all confidential."

"I could get an order from a judge."

"And I could erase them all before you got anywhere near them."

Captain Barnes grinned at him. "You wouldn't do that now, would you? Dr. Clegg said everybody at Lakeshore was going to be so cooperative."

Dr. Ross lowered his eyes. "No, I wouldn't," he said. "I'll have someone box them up for you and sent round to your office this afternoon."

"Thanks, Doctor."

The telephone buzzed. Dr. Ross picked it up, listened and then said, "Okay. I'll be up there right away."

"Anything interesting?" asked Barnes.

"Dr. Clegg wants to talk to me."

"All right, then," said Barnes. "I don't have any more questions right now. But I guess you and I will inevitably be seeing some more of each other."

"The pleasure's all yours," said Dr. Ross.

They left the Titus E. Frobisher wing. Captain Barnes made his way out to the parking lot while Dr. Ross walked along the corridor to the elevators. There were two or three interns in the elevator as it rose to the third floor, and he was conscious of them whispering behind his back. He caught the words "Ross" and "guy that fell off the—"

Dr. Clegg's office was deep-carpeted and quiet, with a heavy mahogany desk and shelves that were lined with his valuable collection of first-edition science books. There was an English carriage clock whirring discreetly on the mantelpiece, and a small bronze statue of a Greek god wrestling with a snake.

"Peter," said Dr. Clegg with unusual intimacy. "Come on in and close the door. Sit down. I was so sorry to hear what happened yesterday."

Dr. Ross sat down in a studded leather chair. He leaned forward slightly, his fingers laced together in his lap. "Thank you," he said. "I'm afraid it was one of those tragic things that we try to avoid and can't."

"Did he fall?" asked Dr. Clegg. "I mean, was it an accidental slip? Or did he let himself go deliberately?"

"I wish I could say. He was reaching out for me. As far as I could see he wanted to be rescued. But then he just plunged over and that was it."

"Come on, Peter," said Dr. Clegg, opening a Delft tobacco jar and taking out his pipe. "You know as well as I do that as far as psychiatry is concerned, no human action ever happens by accident. Lawson committed suicide because he felt guilty."

"With respect, Dr. Clegg, he was my patient and you weren't even there."

"With equal respect, Dr. Ross, I have been talking to Captain Barnes of the police department and Captain Barnes seems to be pretty convinced that Henry had both the ability and the motive to arrange for your apartment to be bombed. He was guilty about Barbara's death, and that's what led him up that building."

"I didn't know we took professional advice from policemen," said Dr. Ross.

"We take professional advice from anyone who's qualified to give it," replied Dr. Clegg, his voice on the edge of sharpness. "The committee and I had a brief meeting here this morning, and we all came to the same conclusion. Considering Lawson's criminal and medical record, and considering his particular knowledge of explosives, it was almost certainly he who was responsible."

"You seem more certain than Captain Barnes himself. He was around to see me this morning and he didn't say anything about closing the case yet."

"Well, he can't, of course, not without further evidence. But between you and me, he said that he was seventy-five percent sure of Lawson's guilt, and he's taken most of his officers off the case."

Dr. Ross sat back. "Well . . ." he said, "I guess there could be something in it."

"Of course there's something in it," said Dr. Clegg. "I know how much you care for your patients, Peter. I know that you always try to protect them and look after them. But it's about time you faced up to the fact that they *are* killers, and that Lawson was a very likely suspect indeed."

"I suppose you're right," said Dr. Ross. "These past two days have been pretty much of a strain."

"I know they have. But the committee and I are full of admiration for the way you've been coping. We all want to say how proud we are of what you tried to do last night at the building site. That kind of thing takes a great deal of dedication and courage. I know we've criticized you in the past, and kept you on your toes, but right now you can count on our full support."

Dr. Ross said, "Thank you."

"You do still wish to carry on the program, I suppose?"

"No question."

"You—uh—you don't mind if you have an audience today?"

"An audience?"

"Dr. Clemens and Dr. Toland have both voiced a desire to watch your therapy at work. They felt that if they could see for themselves that everything was going well, it would reinforce their support for you."

Dr. Ross shrugged. "No, I've no objection to that. Just so long as they observe and don't try to interrupt."

"Oh, they won't do that. They're both very professional ladies."

Dr. Clegg sucked at his pipe, trying to light it up. The aromatic smoke curled across the window, and turned the early sunlight into shining shafts. They reminded Dr. Ross of church.

20

JOHNNY AND BUBBA were sitting side by side on the windowsill in the corridor. From the open door of Johnny's room came the jangling of a rock station on the radio, but neither of them were listening to it. They were too tense and argumentative, too jumpy. Two of their friends had died in forty-eight hours, and nobody could tell them why.

"Dr. Ross shouldn't have let those cops mess around with Henry's head, that's all," Johnny was saying.

"How can you *say* that?" demanded Bubba. "Dr. Ross didn't have no choice. What was he going to do? Refuse to let them question him?"

"All I'm saying is, he said we could trust him, and the next thing we know Henry's taking a dive off the top of a twenty-five-story building."

"Dr. Ross didn't put him up there, did he? Jesus, Johnny, Dr. Ross went up there in a goddamned crane and tried to save him!"

Johnny jumped down from the windowsill. "All right," he said. "Maybe you're right. But what was Henry doing up there in the first place? That guy was scared of falling off of his own shoes!"

The metal door suddenly unlocked, and Dr. Ross came in. He must have heard some of their argument, for he looked first at Johnny and then at Bubba, and said nothing at all.

Johnny turned away and headed back to his room.

"Johnny—" said Dr. Ross.

Johnny paused, without turning around.

"Do you want to talk?" asked Dr. Ross.

"I got nothing to say," Johnny told him sullenly.

"Bubba?" said Dr. Ross.

Bubba climbed down from the windowsill. "I don't feel too good today, Dr. Ross. Reckon I'll lie down for a while."

Dr. Ross watched both of them go. Then, with a dismissive shrug, he continued along the corridor to Laura's room. The door was ajar, but he knocked all the same. Laura said, "Come in."

She was sitting by the window, staring out over the grassy bank that ran around the side of the hospital parking lot. There were two chestnut trees there, nodding in the morning wind. She had a book open in front of her, but she wasn't reading it.

"Laura . . ." said Dr. Ross.

She inclined her head slightly, so that she could see him out of the corner of her eye, but she didn't say anything. He crossed the room and stood beside her, looking out at the view.

"This is a difficult time for all of us, Laura," Dr. Ross said gently. "I liked Henry as much as the rest of you did. Barbara too. But it's very important that we carry on with what we're doing. Do you understand that?"

She nodded.

"We can forget today's treatment if you want to," said Dr. Ross. "We can always catch up on it tomorrow."

"No," she whispered. "I can manage."

"Come along in about five minutes, then," Dr. Ross

told her. "Dr. Toland and Dr. Clemens are going to be watching today to see how you're getting along. You don't mind that, do you?"

"Of course not."

He went to the door, but just as he was about to leave Laura turned in her chair and said, "Dr. Ross— do you really believe that Henry tried to kill you?"

He glanced at her. "No," he said softly, and left.

Dr. Alice Toland and Dr. Clemens were waiting in the hall, drinking coffee from Styrofoam cups. Dr. Ross came briskly in, put down his papers and his progress charts and flicked on a series of switches on his electronic console.

"Good morning, Peter," said Alice Toland, loud enough to make the point that she was peeved at being ignored.

"Laura's just getting herself ready," said Dr. Ross. "Is there any more of that coffee left?"

"You wouldn't want it if there were," remarked Dr. Clemens. "It's positively disgusting."

"I, er, saw Dr. Clegg just now," said Dr. Ross. He kept his head lowered, so that the two doctors were unable to see his face. "I just want to thank you for your support. At a time like this, I really need it."

"Peter—" said Dr. Alice Toland.

He raised his head and looked at her. There was nothing in his expression that invited her to say anything else.

In a little while Laura appeared, petite and pixie-faced, wearing a loose-fitting dress printed with gray flowers. Dr. Ross guided her over to The Box, and she stepped in, but this time he left the door open. He wanted to help her through this treatment session by staying close at hand. After all, with Henry gone and Barbara gone, the success of his remaining three patients' therapy was all the more crucial.

"Today, I'm going to show you a movie," he said in a low voice that Dr. Toland and Dr. Clemens could hardly hear. "There's nothing to be afraid of. It's a very pleasant movie."

Laura, swiveling from side to side on a small chrome stool, gave him a twitchy little smile.

"What I want you to do is help me," said Dr. Ross. "When I run the movie, I want you to describe everything you see in front of you. Do you think you can do that?"

"I'll try, Dr. Ross," she whispered.

"Good. Then shall we start?"

"Okay," she said.

Dr. Ross stepped back to the console, checked the projector indicators and then switched the movie on. There was a soft whirr as the film began to run through the cameras.

At first, Dr. Ross kept well away from Laura, watching her intently with his arms folded and his face emotionless. She turned on her stool and looked at him anxiously over her shoulder, but he described a circle in the air with his finger to tell her that she should turn around again and face the screens.

On the far side of the room, with notepads and pens, Dr. Toland and Dr. Clemens tried to look as serious and as watchful as they could. Dr. Ross glanced around at them and disconcerted them both.

The screens in The Box began to brighten. All around Laura, on three sides, a basketball court appeared. At first it was deserted, but then a door opened and three young basketball players walked in, in red and blue satin shorts and T-shirts, bouncing a ball between them. They fooled around the court for a while, laughing and throwing practice shots at the basket.

"What do you see, Laura?" asked Dr. Ross, coming closer.

"There's, er, boys—playing basketball—"

"Are they happy? Do they make you feel happy?"

"Well, they're kind of—they seem to be having a good time—"

"Do you like them?"

"Sure—they're okay—"

The practice play began to break up. Two of the boys went off to one of the side screens, where they dodged around on their own. The third boy suddenly turned and stared straight at Laura.

"What's happening now, Laura?"

"He's, er, he's looking at me—"

"Do you like him?"

"He's okay—he's coming toward me—I mean he's okay as long as he doesn't—"

"You don't believe he's going to harm you, do you?"

"I just—"

From the other screen, a girl appeared, also dressed in basketball shorts. She was tall, with long blond Scandinavian hair and blue eyes. Her big breasts jiggled sensually under her T-shirt. She padded toward the young man, and they held out their arms for each other. Right in front of Laura's eyes, the two of them embraced and kissed.

Laura was trembling. Dr. Ross was right up close to her now, staring at her. She was trembling and biting at her fingernails.

"Come on, Laura, what do you see? Tell me!"

"A g-girl, and the boy, they're kissing—holding each other—"

"Do they look like they're enjoying it?"

"I think so—it's hard to—"

The blond girl reached under the young basketball player's T-shirt and lifted it up, caressing his bare, muscular chest. Then she stripped his T-shirt right off over his head, so that he was naked from the waist up.

Laura, watching, was making a soft moaning sound
now, a sound which Dr. Ross recognized from previous
treatments.

"Quiet, Laura. Keep quiet and watch. Tell me what
you see."

"He's—he's taking off the girl's T-shirt now—he's
taking it right off—he's running his hands down her
back—"

"Come on, come on."

"He's holding her breasts—squeezing them—rubbing
the nipples with his fingers—she's throwing her head
back—with her eyes closed—like she's—"

"Like she's what, Laura?"

"I don't know—I don't know what she's feeling—
God, I can't stop shaking, Dr. Ross—I can't stop myself shaking—"

"For Christ's sake, Laura, what can you see?"

"I can't—"

"Tell me!"

"She's—the girl's pulling down the boy's shorts—
he's—naked underneath—and she's—touching him—
holding him in her hand—and—no! I can't, Dr. Ross!
I can't!"

"You can, Laura! You have to!"

"I don't want to look any more! I'm scared! I'm
scared, Dr. Ross! I'm *scared!"*

Dr. Ross grabbed Laura's hair and forcibly turned
her head around so that she was facing the screens.
Her face was glistening with cold sweat, and her lower
lip was juddering.

"You have to face it!" shouted Dr. Ross. "It's there,
it's human, and you have to face it!"

"I can't! I can't! I can't!" shrieked Laura.

On the screens in front of her, the girl and the boy
were both naked. The boy was lying on the floor of the
basketball court, and the girl was climbing on top of

him, her legs wide apart. Gracefully, slowly, the girl lowered herself onto the boy, her hand between her thighs to guide him inside her, and they began to make love.

Laura wrenched herself away from Dr. Ross's grasp, pushed him aside from the open door of The Box and ran out into the hall. She collided with Dr. Toland, who had come forward to help her, and when she did so she simply stopped and stood where she was, like a toy robot that had reached the end of the room and couldn't go any further. She didn't cry out. She just stood there, her face contorted with fear, her fists clenched in front of her.

Dr. Clemens snapped, "Turn that thing off!"

Dr. Ross walked slowly across to the console, located the switch and turned the projectors off. The movie faded away into darkness. He stood by the console without moving, staring at a point somewhere just beyond the edge of The Box.

"Can you get her a blanket, please?" said Dr. Toland. "She's shaking like a leaf."

Dr. Clemens looked around. Dr. Ross, without saying a word, picked up a plaid traveling rug from one of the chairs and tossed it over.

"Come on, honey," said Dr. Toland. "You're going to be okay now. Everything's going to be all right."

Dr. Clemens put her arm around Laura and led her to the door. Laura was white-faced and shuffling, and with every step she moaned, as if she'd been physically hurt.

Dr. Toland came across to the console. Dr. Ross watched her coming, with obvious indifference.

"That was one hell of a display you put on there," said Dr. Toland coldly.

He raised an eyebrow. "That was a normal part of Laura's treatment."

"Normal? Did you see what it did to her?"

"Of course. But she's a damned sight better now than she was a month ago. A month ago, she couldn't even be in the same room as a man."

"Implosive therapy," said Dr. Toland, shaking her head. "Or, if you can't cure them, kill them. That's really unbelievable."

Dr. Ross sat down, reached across for his notes and began to write up his report. "You shouldn't really criticize what you don't understand," he said flatly.

"I understand that I saw the most obscene display I've ever witnessed in all my years in professional psychiatry."

"You saw Henry's vertigo treatment. You've seen what I do to Johnny and Bubba. Why should this be any worse?"

"It's worse because it's an affront to human dignity," snapped Dr. Toland.

"No, it's not," said Dr. Ross, glancing toward the door to make sure that Dr. Clemens had taken Laura out. "It's worse because it's erotic. It's worse because it offends Dr. Toland's personal sense of sexual decorum. You were always anxious when it came to bedtime, Alice, and now your anxiety is beginning to peep out from under your professional skirts like a cheap underslip. Maybe you should take some of this treatment yourself."

"You don't have to—" she began, but then she stopped herself.

"I don't have to *what?* Hurt you any more than I've hurt you already? Is that it? Well, tell me, Alice, just how much do I have to hurt you to make you understand that I *will* be friends, but I *won't* be harassed."

She stood beside him for a long while without speaking. Then she said, "Can't anybody reach you, in any way at all?"

He looked up. "Of course they can. I'm not a machine, Alice. But right at this moment there is only one thing I really care about and that is this therapy program, and my patients."

"Yes," she said in a hoarse whisper. "I thought it was."

She turned around and left him at the console, still writing up his report. He didn't even raise his eyes when she slammed the door to the hall.

21

DR. CLEMENS TOOK Laura straight back to her room and through to the the small white-tiled bathroom which she had previously shared with Barbara. While Laura sat on the cork-topped stool shivering, Dr. Clemens turned on the faucets and filled up the tub.

"This is the oldest therapy in the world," she told Laura. "A nice relaxing bath. It's good for the circulation and it's good for the soul. You'll feel cleaner afterward too, if you know what I mean."

Laura nodded dumbly. Dr. Clemens tested the water with her hand and then said, "That's fine. You have a good soak and call for Dr. Toland or me when you're through."

"Thank you, Doctor," said Laura.

"I'll have a word with Dr. Clegg," said Dr. Clemens. "Maybe we'll see if we can't—well, *modify* your treatment a little."

Laura said, "I have to do it, though, don't I? If I don't do it, I'll never get better."

Dr. Clemens laid a hand on her shoulder. "There are all kinds of clinical definitions of 'better,' my girl, just as there are all kinds of definitions of psychological normality. None of them are worth much. All that's worth anything to you is inner peace, along with a reasonable amount of stability and freedom from irrational fear."

Laura started to unbutton her dress. Dr. Clemens said, "You'll be fine for the moment, anyway. I'm just glad that Dr. Toland and I were there to help."

The doctor went out and closed the door behind her. Laura undressed, hanging her dress and her underwear on the hook at the side of the mirror, and then she opened the door and peeked out, just to make sure there was nobody out there. The police department had insisted that none of the patients' rooms should have locks, in case of suicide attempts.

Still shaking a little, she eased herself into the warm water of the bathtub. Dr. Clemens had been right. It was soothing and relaxing, and as she sat down and let it flow over her shoulders, it began to ease away her shivers.

What she had seen in The Box had frightened her. It had brought back in one horrifying surge all the hysteria of being thrown down on those old tires and raped again and again. But, somehow, she knew that she was going to have to go on facing up to those feelings. If she didn't, she was going to end up as some awkward and dried-up old spinster with nothing to show for her life but years of loneliness and a prison record.

Kind though Dr. Clemens and Dr. Toland were, she still believed that Dr. Ross had the key to making her better.

She was lying there thinking about Dr. Ross and watching the steam fade away from the windows when the door handle clicked. She stared at it, unsure if she had heard anything or not. But then it clicked again, and to Laura's horror it slowly began to turn.

Frozen with fear, suddenly chilled again in spite of the warmth of the water, she called out, "Who's there? Is that you, Dr. Clemens?"

There was no answer. The door handle turned a fraction more.

Laura climbed out of the water, her eyes fixed on the door, and reached for her towel. She wrapped it around her waist and circled across the bathroom, biting her nails in anxiety. She struck the cork-topped stool with her knee, and for a moment her attention was diverted.

The bathroom door opened. Laura's eyes widened and she clutched the towel even more tightly around herself.

"Hello, Laura," said a soft voice.

"No," said Laura. "Please!"

"This isn't going to hurt, Laura. Not like all that treatment. This is going to be the easiest thing you ever had to do."

"No!" shrieked Laura.

She backed away, slipped on the wet tiles of the floor and teetered over the bathtub. The towel was abruptly torn away from her body, and she was given a hard shove which sent her splashing into the water. She screamed, took a mouthful of hot bathwater, bubbled and screamed again. But the towel was wrapped around her head like a wet hangman's hood, and she was forced under the water again by arms that were stronger and harder than she was able to resist.

Inside her mind, there was nothing but explosive panic. She felt as if her brain was going to burst. Then she took a deep breath, and felt the bathwater pouring into her lungs. The last thing she saw was the orange color of the hospital towel over her eyes.

She rolled in the water, drowned. The bathroom door was opened, held for a moment and then closed.

22

BUBBA AND JOHNNY stood at the back of the crowd in the corridor, trying to see what was happening. Right now, though, the two convicted killers were being jostled out of the way. The corridor was crowded with police, hospital staff, nurses and paramedics. From inside Laura's room, the coroner's photographers sent out flashes like summer lightning.

"I don't believe it," said Bubba. "I just don't believe it!"

The security guard was standing not far away, swinging his whistle on the end of its lanyard. Johnny tugged his sleeve and said, "Somebody told us Laura was dead. Is that true?"

"That's right," the security guard told him. "Drowned in the bathtub."

Bubba and Johnny pushed forward through the crowd. "I've got to see this," said Bubba desperately. "I've got to see what happened."

They struggled through to Laura's door, but a policeman held them back. "Keep back, will ya? They're bringing her out in a minute."

"I have to see her," insisted Bubba. "This guy and me, we're her friends. Tell Dr. Ross that we're here."

"Dr. Ross ain't here," said the policeman. "Now, will you just ease back along the corridor?"

"They're out looking for Dr. Ross," somebody said.

"You mean he doesn't *know* yet?" asked Johnny. "Oh, Jesus, this is going to crucify him."

"What happened?" Bubba asked one of the Lakeshore nurses. "Do you know? Or won't they tell you?"

"The way I heard it, she collapsed in the treatment room," the nurse told him. "Dr. Clemens and Dr. Toland brought her up here to take a bath . . . just to calm her down, you know? They told the matron to go take a look at her, make sure she was all right . . . but when matron went in there, she was drowned."

"Oh, Jesus," said Johnny. "Oh, Jesus, that's three."

"When did this happen?" asked Bubba.

"Who knows? An hour ago, maybe less."

The policeman suddenly pushed them all back from Laura's doorway. "Get back!" he yelled. "Get back all of you, or I'll clear this whole damned corridor!"

Johnny turned around, instantly resentful at being shoved. But Bubba grabbed the front of his shirt and pulled him bodily through the crowd, until they were standing by the outer door, well out of the way of the police.

"Goddamn cops, throwing their weight around," said Johnny viciously.

"Cool it, will you?" Bubba told him. "It ain't going to do either of us any good if you start upsetting the law."

"What are we going to do?" asked Johnny.

"I don't know," said Bubba in a low voice. "But I can tell you one thing for sure. If anybody did this to Laura, I'm going to take them apart."

"Maybe *nobody* did it," said Johnny.

"What does that mean?"

"Well, maybe she fainted, or had a heart attack."

"Oh, yeah?"

"Yeah. It's probably death from natural causes. It happens all the time in prisons. One old guy I knew, back in the state pen, all he did was choke on a baked bean, and he suffocated. They were rousting us for days, thinking we'd strangled him."

"A baked bean, huh?" said Bubba. He thought for a while. "Well, I guess she could have slipped and hit her head."

"Something like that," said Johnny.

Bubba's eyes filled with tears. He clamped his hand over his mouth to stop himself from sobbing.

"That poor kid," he said, after a minute or two. "That poor damned lonesome kid."

There was a burst of noise, and two policemen came out of Laura's doorway, immediately followed by two ambulance attendants with a rolling stretcher. The stretcher was sped down the corridor, past Bubba and Johnny, but not so quickly that they couldn't see the small form that was strapped onto it and covered with a red blanket. The security door was held open while police, ambulance men and medics all hurried after the corpse.

It was like a ridiculous race that had already been lost.

Pushing his way against the tide of people came Sergeant Wheeler. His face was red and sweating, and he took off his hat to wipe his forehead with his handkerchief. He let the last of the people go by, and then he crossed over to Laura's room. Captain Barnes was just coming out, with Dr. Toland and Dr. Radetzki, the police surgeon.

"Well?" barked Captain Barnes. "Have you located Ross?"

Sergeant Wheeler shook his head. "They say he hasn't answered his bleeper. But they did say that—"

"You mean you haven't found him yet?" demanded Captain Barnes. "What are we running here—a police force or a goddamned Girl Scout patrol?"

"If he's not answering his bleeper, he's at the rink," said Dr. Toland, quietly.

"That's what his call service told me," Sergeant Wheeler said pugnaciously. "You just didn't give me the chance to finish."

"Well, if he's at the rink, go get him," said Captain Barnes. "Did you reach Dr. Clemens?"

"Yes, sir. She's on her way over here now."

"Okay. What are you waiting for? The Day of Judgment? Go get Ross!"

Sergeant Wheeler hurried away again. The crowds in the corridor were dwindling away now, and the security guard had taken up his position at the door to screen everybody who left. One of the police officers came up to Captain Barnes and said, "Everything all right, sir? I think we're pretty well finished up in the bathroom."

Captain Barnes looked around. "Yes," he said. "But there's one more thing. Go find Johnny Venuti and Bernard King. I want them in here right now for questioning."

"Okay, sir. That's Bernard King over there."

Captain Barnes turned around. Bubba was standing on his own, and it was immediately and glaringly obvious that Johnny wasn't with him. Captain Barnes stared at him for a long, long moment, his eyes as hard and uncompromising as fractured flints.

"I don't suppose you have the remotest idea what's happened to your friend Venuti, do you, Mr. King?" Captain Barnes asked sarcastically.

Bubba shook his head from side to side. "Sure don't, Captain Barnes, sir."

"Well," said Captain Barnes. "I've heard of the murderer returning to the scene of the crime, but this is the first time I've heard of him leaving the scene of the crime along with the victim. Officer, I want an APB on Johnny Venuti right away. He's broke, he doesn't have an overcoat and he's as nutty as a fruitcake. They shouldn't find it hard to track him down."

The officer unfastened his handcuffs from his belt and approached Bubba cautiously. Bubba obligingly turned around and offered his wrists. "Just so long as you don't bring no snakes near me, I'll do whatever you want." He grinned.

23

THE ICE RINK was frigid and gloomy, like the entrance hall to Valhalla. The rows and rows of empty seats were deep in darkness, and out on the ice only the smallest spotlights picked out the single skater who was weaving and turning between imaginary opponents, expertly chasing a hockey puck across the white, scored surface.

Sergeant Wheeler came slowly down the steps of the auditorium as the skater performed a high-speed slide up to the goal and slammed the puck straight into the net. He stood where he was and clapped.

"Nice goal, Dr. Ross!" Wheeler called out. His breath smoked in the chill from the ice. His voice echoed.

Dr. Ross skated backward in a circle, and then slid across to the barrier. "A fan, huh?" he asked breathlessly.

"That's a mean shot you've got there," said Wheeler. "You've got what those sportswriters call the killer instinct."

Dr. Ross cleared his throat. "If you're going to win, you can't hold anything back. That's the whole secret of success."

"I used to play defense," said Wheeler. "Mind you, that was a few years ago now."

"Why didn't you stick with it?" asked Dr. Ross. "I would have thought ice hockey was good exercise for a cop. Helps you develop those beating-up muscles."

Sergeant Wheeler didn't answer, but gazed out across the ice with an expression that immediately alerted Dr. Ross that something was wrong.

"You didn't come here to talk about ice hockey, did you?" he asked the sergeant.

Wheeler looked him straight in the eye. "No, Dr. Ross, I didn't. Captain Barnes wants to see you."

"Is it anything urgent? Or do I have time to finish my practice?"

"It's urgent. Well, that's if you think that Laura Adams drowning in her own bathtub is urgent."

Dr. Ross stared at him.

"I'm sorry," said Sergeant Wheeler. "It only happened an hour ago. I just came from there—as soon as I found out where you were."

"Laura's drowned?" asked Dr. Ross, his voice tight in his throat. "Are you serious?"

"I wouldn't put you on, Dr. Ross. I saw her myself."

"What the hell happened? Does anyone know? Did anyone see her?"

"The matron found her. Nobody knows what happened yet. They may have found out more by the time we get back to the hospital."

"Laura," whispered Dr. Ross. "I can't believe it."

Sergeant Wheeler was embarrassed. "I'm sorry," he said. "I know you've had a pretty tough time over the past couple of days. But it would help if you could get yourself dressed and come as soon as you can. Captain Barnes isn't in a very patient kind of a mood today, you know?"

Dr. Ross ran his hand through his thick, curly hair.

"Okay," he said in an unsteady voice. "Give me a couple of minutes to change, and I'll meet you outside."

They drove back to Lakeshore Hospital in silence. Every now and then there was a garbled burst of police messages on the radio, but Sergeant Wheeler turned the volume right down, so that there was nothing but the tiniest of voices calling for back-up for a two-eleven on Quincy, or for officers to proceed to Fairview Park to check up on a suspected indecent exposure.

"Great job you have," said Dr. Ross, nodding toward the radio as they turned at last into the hospital parking lot.

"You cure 'em, but we have to catch 'em," said Sergeant Wheeler. "You get used to it, after the first fifteen years."

There was a crowd of newspaper reporters and television cameramen around the hospital entrance. But Sergeant Wheeler took Dr. Ross by the arm and led him through the chaos of shouted questions and jostling notebooks and bobbing cameras as if he was a child. Sergeant Wheeler may have been out of condition, but he still had the strength to drag a witness through a melee of newsmen, or a suspect out of a downtown bar. They pushed their way through the hospital doors, and two uniformed policemen closed the doors behind them.

"Fame at last, huh?" said Sergeant Wheeler. "There's nothing that attracts the buzzards better than a multiple homicide."

"You really think it's homicide?" asked Dr. Ross.

Sergeant Wheeler took out a stick of gum, pushed it into his mouth and started to chew. "You really think it's coincidence?" he retorted.

Dr. Alice Toland was waiting for him by the doors of the Titus E. Frobisher wing. Her hair was mussed up, and she looked tense and distraught.

"Peter . . ." she said. "I have to talk to you."

Dr. Ross stopped. He was grinding his teeth again, and that small muscle was moving in his cheek.

Dr. Toland said, "I just want to tell you how bad I feel about Laura."

"Sure," said Dr. Ross. "I understand."

"The thing is, Peter, I may be responsible for what happened. I left it all to Dr. Clemens, and I didn't bother to go back and check on Laura myself. If only I had done . . ."

Dr. Ross lowered his eyes. He found himself looking at the aluminum doorplate along the bottom of the swing doors. There were two screws missing, and he wondered why he hadn't noticed them before. "You can't blame yourself, Alice," he said abstractedly.

"But I do," she told him, stepping nearer. "I should have gone to check her myself."

"Do you know what happened?" asked Dr. Ross.

"Nobody does, not exactly. I talked to Dr. Clegg and he said that it was probably an accident. But an accident? Three patients out of five?"

Dr. Ross stared at her. "What do you mean, three patients out of five?"

"Well, don't you think their deaths are connected?" asked Dr. Toland. "How normal is it for three people out of a social group of five to die within forty-eight hours?"

"I don't know," said Dr. Ross. "You're the analyst. You tell me."

Dr. Toland spread her arms wide, in temper and frustration. "It's not very normal at all!" she said. "You know that as well as I do!"

"Don't you believe in misfortune?" asked Dr. Ross. "Don't you believe in coincidence? These patients were always more at risk than any other social group of five, because of their record. They're killers, and they're all suffering from phobias. I'd hate to think what kind of a premium they'd have to pay on a life policy."

"Laura's dead!" said Dr. Toland. "Laura's dead, and that's all you can say? For God's sake, Peter, what makes you work?"

"Caring for my patients, that's what makes me work," said Dr. Ross. "Now I think I have to go see Captain Barnes."

"Peter," she said, "there's something wrong. I feel there's something wrong."

"Christ," he told her, "you have the coldest, most analytical mind I've ever come across. And now you're having feelings?"

"Peter, there's something going on here—something deeper—"

"Alice," he said, "the last thing I need right now is your dubious services as an analyst. Sergeant Wheeler, let's go."

Dr. Toland caught his arm. She tried to look him directly in the face, but he turned away.

"Peter," she said, "what's happened to you?"

"What do you mean, what's happened to me?"

"You're different. Changed. You were never like this with me before."

"That was before."

She wouldn't let him go. "You're so—I don't know, *aggressive*."

Dr. Ross looked at her at last, and his eyes were expressionless. "I'm not aggressive, Alice, I'm defensive. I'm trying to protect the last thing I've got that means anything. This phobia program. Now, get off my case, will you? I have to talk to the police."

Dr. Toland released his arm reluctantly and stepped back. Dr. Ross pushed his way through the swinging doors, with Sergeant Wheeler close behind him. As he disappeared, Sergeant Wheeler turned around to Dr.

Toland and gave her a shrug. It didn't mean much, except *I'm sorry, Doctor, that's the way things are.*

As Dr. Ross approached his office, he could hear Captain Barnes snapping away at Bubba. He caught the words "you're lying, of course," and then he walked into his office and confronted both of them. Captain Barnes, who had been sitting on the edge of his desk, immediately stood up. Bubba, confused and sweating, got up from his chair and moved behind Dr. Ross like a child seeking protection.

"What's going on here?" asked Dr. Ross.

Captain Barnes pointed to Bubba. "That son of a bitch wouldn't know the truth if it hit him in the face with a wet facecloth. He's lying, but he won't admit it."

"What would he lie about?" said Dr. Ross, walking around his desk.

"He knows where Johnny Venuti is, but he won't tell me," said Barnes, with a false grin. "He thinks it's in all of our interests if I don't find out."

"Johnny? He's here, isn't he?" asked Dr. Ross.

"Oh, no!" said Captain Barnes. "While we were fishing your phobic lady friend out of the tub, he took off. And in my book that narrows the suspects down to just one."

"So you think it was a homicide, do you?" Dr. Ross wanted to know. "You don't believe it was just another accident?"

"Not a hope," said Captain Barnes. "The coroner called me five minutes ago and expressed the expert opinion that Laura Adams had been forcibly held under the water until she drowned."

"It wasn't me, Dr. Ross," said Bubba urgently. "I swear to God it wasn't me. I wouldn't do that for nothing!"

Dr. Ross stared at him. Bubba's face was twitching,

and he was almost as upset as he was during one of his treatments in The Box.

"If Johnny didn't do anything, why did he run?" asked Dr. Ross in a level voice.

"He was frightened, I guess. They brought Laura's body out, and there was a whole crowd of people around . . . and he just took off. . . ."

"We have an APB out on him," put in Captain Barnes dryly.

"He'll come back, Dr. Ross," said Bubba. "He's just upset, that's all. He didn't do nothing, any more than I did. We were just playing cards like we always do, and suddenly there was all this screaming and yelling, and they told us that Laura was dead. . . ."

"You seriously believe that?" asked Captain Barnes. "You seriously believe that a prime murder suspect is going to come strolling back into the arms of the law?"

Bubba raised his head defiantly. "He may have took off, Captain, but he didn't do nothing, and that means he's going to be back."

Captain Barnes looked across at Sergeant Wheeler and shook his head. "Can you believe these people, Sergeant? A guy who slaughtered a little old lady for no reason at all wants us to sit back on our butts and wait because another guy who smashed the brains out of a prison warder for no reason at all is bound to return to his cell of his own free will."

"These aren't cells, Captain," said Dr. Ross tersely.

"I don't care if they're suites at the Plaza," retorted Captain Barnes. "Johnny Venuti won't come back because he's suspected of homicide."

"He's anxious, that's all," said Dr. Ross. "All of these deaths are bound to create a stress situation . . . and on people who are under stress already the effect is devastating."

Captain Barnes looked as if he was about to say something sharp and sarcastic in return, but instead he simply buttoned up his coat.

"You can think what you like, Doctor," he said after a while. "You're an educated man, a well-respected expert in your own field. You're entitled to your own opinion."

Dr. Ross paused for a moment and then he pushed a button on his desk telephone. "Reception?" he said. "This is Dr. Ross here. Tell the message service I'm going out for the rest of the day in my car . . . so they can reach me on the car phone. After that, they can probably find me at Miss St. Clair's apartment. That'll be sometime after six. No, make that seven."

Captain Barnes stared at Dr. Ross inquisitively. Dr. Ross said, "I'm going out to look for Johnny. Any objections?"

"Not if you call me when you've found him."

Dr. Ross went over to Bubba and laid his hand on his shoulder. "Listen, Bubba, he said quietly. "I want you to stay here and I want you to stay cool. I know the problems, but do you think you can do that?"

Bubba nodded. "You'll bring him back, won't you, Dr. Ross? He didn't do nothing, I swear."

"I'll bring him back," promised Dr. Ross.

Captain Barnes went to talk to Dr. Clegg for a few minutes, so when Dr. Ross walked out into the hospital parking lot, Sergeant Wheeler was standing by their dark green Bonneville alone, assiduously chewing gum.

"How long ago did Barnes put out that APB on Johnny Venuti?" asked Dr. Ross.

"An hour. Something like that."

"Any news yet?"

Sergeant Wheeler shook his head. "I just checked in. Nothing yet."

"Could you hold it off for an hour?"

Sergeant Wheeler's jaws slowed down. "What do you mean, hold it off for an hour?"

"Give me an hour's break. Cancel the APB until five o'clock."

"I don't have the authority to do that. And in any case, why the hell should I?"

Dr. Ross smiled. "Because you owe me one."

"What do you mean?" said Wheeler, crinkling up his nose in doubt.

"I talked to Henry Lawson on the building, remember . . . and before he fell he told me what happened when you and Barnes interrogated him. . . ."

"Nothing happened! What are you talking about?"

Dr. Ross was stretching his luck now. But he knew that Henry wouldn't have screamed those two words *"Barnes"* and *"chair"* if the detectives hadn't been doing something to frighten him. And why the hell had Henry climbed all the way up that building, unless Barnes and Wheeler had scared him more than his phobia of heights?

"I'm talking about the chair," said Dr. Ross. "That's what I'm talking about."

Sergeant Wheeler didn't answer for a long time. He just kept on moving his gum from one side of his mouth to the other.

"The chair?" coaxed Dr. Ross.

Sergeant Wheeler glanced over his shoulder. Then he said, "It wasn't my idea. It was Captain Barnes's."

"That doesn't make any difference. The commissioner would find you equally guilty. And from what I hear, pounding the beat in Cleveland isn't as much fun as it used to be."

Sergeant Wheeler glanced at his watch. "Okay," he said tersely. "I'll give you fifteen minutes."

"Fifteen? Make it a half-hour."

"This is blackmail, you know. That's a big offense."

"Sure," nodded Dr. Ross. "And so is mistreating a suspect during interrogation."

"You got twenty minutes," said Sergeant Wheeler. He reached inside the Bonneville for his radio transmitter and at the same time flapped his hand at Dr. Ross to tell him to get moving. As Dr. Ross walked briskly toward his Porsche, he heard Sergeant Wheeler saying, "Venuti. That's right. Seems like there's been some kind of misunderstanding."

What he didn't see was Sergeant Wheeler's thumb on the microphone's OFF button.

24

HE WAS DRIVING along Lorain Avenue, just crossing the Cuyahoga River, when his car phone buzzed. He slowed down behind a heavy haulage truck and picked it up.

"Ross here. Yes. That's right."

The call service girl said, "There's somebody wants to talk to you from a telephone booth. . . . He won't give his name . . . but he says he's a friend."

"Okay," said Dr. Ross. "I think I know who it is. Put him through."

There was a crackling sound, and then Dr. Ross heard Johnny Venuti say, *"Dr. Ross—Dr. Ross—is that you?"*

"Johnny? Where are you speaking from?"

"I'm in a phone booth, just outside of a drugstore on Clark."

Dr. Ross glanced at the clock on the Porsche's dash. "I'll tell you what, Johnny. Go to Miss St. Clair's apartment—you remember Miss St. Clair?—go to her apartment, Number Seven Newburgh Street. That's close to the zoo. She lives on the top floor. Make sure nobody sees you when you go in. I'll meet you there in a little while."

"Dr. Ross—" said Johnny.

"What is it?"

"You don't think they're going to kill all of us, do you, Dr. Ross? The way they did Henry and Laura and Barbara?"

"Johnny," said Dr. Ross, "we've had three tragic accidents. The police say they're all connected but I'm not so sure. If Henry's death is anything to go by, then the police themselves aren't above suspicion. So all I'm asking you to do is keep clear of the police for now—watch out for police cars and anybody who's obviously hanging around keeping a lookout—and make your way around to Miss St. Clair's as fast as you can. And, listen, there's one thing more—"

Johnny waited until Dr. Ross had finished, and then he said, *"All right, Dr. Ross. I got you. And—well, thanks."*

"You don't have to thank me, Johnny. We've been fighting on the same side for a long time now."

Dr. Ross put the car phone back in its cradle, glanced in his rear-view mirror and pulled out into the late afternoon traffic. He was at Lorain and West 73rd now, and he turned south. A few blocks along, he picked up the car phone again and asked the operator to put him through to Jenny.

The phone rang for a long time before she answered. Even then, she simply said, "St. Clair."

"Jenny? This is Peter. Listen, I need a favor."

"A favor? What kind of a favor?"

"It's Johnny Venuti. He slipped out of the hospital this afternoon. He called me a minute ago and I told him it was okay if he went around to your place."

"He slipped out of the hospital? You mean, he escaped?"

"That's right, he escaped."

"Is anything wrong? You sound funny."

Dr. Ross slowed down for a set of traffic signals. "Maybe I am a little off balance. The reason Johnny broke out was because Laura Adams was found drowned in her bathtub this afternoon."

"Laura? I can't believe it!"

"I couldn't believe it, either. The police are trying to make out it's a homicide, but the way it looks right now she just hit her head and drowned. But, anyway, Captain Barnes has been pretty heavy on the idea of Bubba and Johnny being responsible—you know what he thinks about my pet killers—and Johnny was so frightened he made a break."

"He's not—"

"He's not what? Homicidal? Is that what you mean?"

"Well, I was just wondering."

"Jenny, would I send anyone around to stay at your place if I thought they were a genuine killer?"

There was a pause. Then she said, "I guess not. I'm sorry."

"He'll be around in about ten minutes, I guess," said Dr. Ross. "He was calling from a phone booth on Clark."

"It sounds like he was desperate," said Jenny, trying to be composed.

"Yes," said Dr. Ross.

There was another pause, longer. "I'll see you later, then," said Jenny.

"Okay," said Dr. Ross. "I love you."

He replaced the receiver. He had reached the intersection of West 73rd and Ridge now, and he turned down Ridge. The street lights were beginning to flicker on, and the sky was dramatically dark to the east, although the western horizon was still quite light. He drove slowly and methodically, obedient to the speed limit and the traffic signals, and aware of the cars and buses around him. It was as if he felt a need to conform to the rules, and to the society which had treated his phobia program with such suspicion.

Alice had been right. Three out of five. It made him feel as if the firm ground of his whole career had suddenly opened under his feet and left him perched on the crumbling remains of his two least promising patients, Johnny and Bubba. There wasn't any doubt now that Dr. Clegg would call a halt to the phobia project, and that Townsend Cereals would expect the balance of their finance back. Dr. Ross rubbed the side of his back with his hand, as if he was trying to relieve the tension he was feeling. He sometimes wished he was a drinker. He could go and get smashed out of his mind and forget the whole damned thing.

He suddenly found the street lights had turned blurry, and when he reached up and touched his eyes, he realized he was crying.

25

Jenny had been expecting the knock on her door, but it still surprised her when it came. She had been smoothing the wing of a clay penguin—the corporate symbol of a frozen food company—and she stopped with her arm raised and a faint trickle of water running down the side of the sculpture. She set down her tools and walked to the door, wiping her hands on her striped overall.

"Yes?" she said.

"It's me, Johnny Venuti."

She licked her lips. Then, taking a breath, she opened the door on the chain and peered out. Standing in the darkness of the upper landing was thin, pale young man with greased-back hair and a worn leather jacket. He was older than she remembered, and whiter, but he was still the same Johnny Venuti she'd seen in those black and white photographs in Peter's files. She released the chain on the door and let him in.

He stepped to one side and stood by her bookshelves, looking nervous and embarrassed.

"I shouldn't think Dr. Ross will be long," said Jenny. She walked across to the clay penguin and carefully arranged a damp towel over it. "He called me to say you were coming."

"Oh, yeah?" said Johnny. "That's good. That's real good."

"Listen," said Jenny, "do you want a drink? A cup of coffee, maybe?"

Johnny waved his hands. "I'll be okay. I'm just a little wound up, that's all."

"Dr. Ross told me about Laura," said Jenny.

"Laura, can you imagine it?" Johnny asked her, agitated. He kept on tugging the zipper of his jacket up and down. "She drowned in the tub. Drowned! And all the cops were around saying it was Bubba or me. I mean Bernard. But that was nuts. Do you know how nuts that was? We were both playing cards ever since— I don't know. But Bubba didn't do it, and neither did I. The whole thing's insane."

Johnny took a deep breath, to try and calm himself. Then, while Jenny cleared up her tools, he walked around her sculptures, looking at them closely. The only piece he turned away from was the reflecting metal sculpture. The white, haunted face that looked back at him was too frightening.

"These yours?" he asked Jenny.

"That's right. I'm a sculptor."

"Pretty good. You ever done one of the doc?"

"Not yet," she smiled. "I haven't been able to get him to sit still for long enough."

Johnny let out a quick, nervous laugh. "That's right. Right. That's the doc for you."

He suddenly started to shake, and he had to reach out and grab Jenny's side table for support. His face was the color of a crumpled-up newspaper, and sweat was running down his neck.

"I don't feel so good," he said, unsteadily. "I feel sick."

Jenny said, "The bathroom's—"

"No—no thanks. I'm not that kind of sick. Listen,

just let me sit down, could you? I'll be okay in a minute."

Jenny took his arm and guided him over to her flower-printed settee. He sat down stiffly, and stayed there with his head held erect and his teeth chattering.

"Would you like some coffee?" she asked him. "It wouldn't be any trouble."

"I'm fine. Fine. Really I am. It's just the whole thing's been——"

"Yes," said Jenny sympathetically. "I can imagine it has."

"Sure, the doc must have told you about it," Johnny said. "It's kind of weird, huh? All of us getting killed or dying or falling off of buildings like this."

"It must make you feel very frightened," said Jenny, sitting on the arm of the settee and reaching her hand out to him.

Johnny stared at her hand as if he didn't know what it was. As suspicious as Bubba, looking at a snake. "The thing is," he said, "I just can't work out what the hell's happening. I mean, if it was somebody's relative, the wife or the husband of somebody that one of us killed, you'd think they'd just kill the person who blew away their own particular loved one and leave it at that. Why try to knock off all of us?"

"Maybe it's somebody who hates everything the phobia program stands for," suggested Jenny.

"Well, I thought about that," said Johnny. "I thought about some of those doctors up at Lakeshore. Dr. Clegg, you know—he's always saying how great the program is, but you can bet whatever you like that he'd do anything to get it off the premises. It's been too much of a hassle for him ever since it started. Then there's Dr. Clemens. She don't like it either. In fact, she hates it so much she made a point of being around when Laura took her last treatment."

Johnny couldn't stay sitting any longer, and he got up from the settee and started to strut nervously around the room.

"There's Captain Barnes too. He's been dead set against it all along. He fought tooth and nail to stop the program even getting started. Now, he's snooping around the hospital in person, handling the whole case on his own, even though he's a captain. I ask you— what's a captain doing on a case like this?"

"You missed somebody," said Jenny.

"Jesus, Miss St. Clair, I missed *everybody*. It could have been any one of hundreds of people. And the way they died—Barbara and Henry and Laura—you couldn't even tell if the same person did it."

"You still missed somebody. Somebody important. Somebody who might have had a personal motive for stopping the program."

Johnny stopped on the other side of the room, and frowned at Jenny through the heart-shaped hole in the center of her stainless-steel sculpture.

"You're not talking about—?"

"Why not?"

Johnny turned his head away. "I don't know why not. For some reason, she's always seemed too obvious."

"Don't obvious people sometimes turn out to be exactly what they always appeared to be?"

"I guess so," said Johnny uncomfortably. "I really thought it was her, to begin with. I mean, she hasn't ever tried to hide the way she feels about the doc. You could really say that she's got the hots for him. But, I don't know, murder. . . . Somehow she doesn't look like the murdering type."

Jenny stared at him. "Do you think *you* look the murdering type? Yet you are."

Johnny thought about that for a moment, and then went across to the window. There was something about

the way he was standing that told Jenny he wasn't too
enthusiastic about talking anymore.

He said dully, "The doc's a hell of a time."

"I'm sure he's getting here as quick as he can," said
Jenny.

Johnny peered into the street below. "There's a car
pulling up outside now. . . ." he said. "It don't look
like no Porsche, though. It looks more like a—Christ,
it's the cops! It's Barnes! Oh, Christ, I've had it!"

Jenny ran to the window and looked down at the
street. Barnes's dark green Bonneville had drawn up
underneath a street lamp, and Barnes and Wheeler were
just climbing out of it. Across the road, a black-and-
white had arrived, its red lights flashing, and it was
obvious from the reflections of other red lights in the
windows along the street that the whole neighborhood
had been blocked off.

Johnny was already at the door, turning the lock and
releasing the safety chain. Jenny ran back and tried to
close the door so that he couldn't get out, but he pushed
her roughly aside.

"Johnny!" she shouted. "Wait for Dr. Ross! Please!"

"Forget it," Johnny told her. "I have to get out of
here, and that's all!"

There was nothing she could do to stop him. He ran
across the hallway and rattled the doorknob of the jani-
tor's cupboard before moving across to the next apartment and trying that. Every door was firmly locked,
and there was no way out. Already, Johnny could hear
footsteps on the staircase and the sound of Captain
Barnes's voice. He looked back toward Jenny in total
panic, and she tried to beckon him back into her apartment, but he was too scared and now he was running
for his life.

He dragged back the sliding door of the elevator with
a loud clashing noise. The elevator had jammed again,

between Jenny's floor and the floor below. Johnny craned his neck and looked up the darkened shaft. He could faintly see the light of evening straining through a small access door from the roof. If he could clamber up the inside of the shaft, then maybe he could get away before Barnes had realized where he'd gone. On the roof, he could run along the length of the block, and escape the police cordon altogether.

Coughing, Johnny lifted himself on to the roof of the jammed elevator car, causing the latticework door for toe holds. Once he was up there, he leaned back and closed the outer gates behind him, so that Barnes wouldn't immediately see where he'd disappeared. He could hear Barnes complaining, "That's psychologists for you. They're all nuts. They seem to think that you can learn from life out of a book."

Johnny stepped across the roof of the elevator, reaching out to grasp the greasy steel cables for balance. There was a juddering, shaking sound, and the elevator seemed to shift under his feet. For ten tense seconds Johnny stayed rock still, holding his breath, praying that Captain Barnes hadn't heard him. It was so damned close and claustrophobic in this shaft that it was all he could do to stop himself from calling out to the police to arrest him straight away and take him out into the fresh air. He closed his eyes for a moment and he could picture himself inside Dr. Ross's Box, with those back-projected walls closing in and closing in, until he felt as if every ounce of air was being squeezed out of his lungs.

Captain Barnes must have reached the second floor now. Johnny could hear him saying, "Of course Ross has to date some sculptress who lives on the top floor. Have you tried that damned elevator again, Wheeler?"

Johnny heard a clicking sound in the elevator system's wiring as Sergeant Wheeler pressed the button on the second floor. At first, nothing happened, but then the elevator car beneath Johnny's feet gave an abrupt lurch, and the steel cable started to run through his fingers. He was only holding onto the wire for a second, but it took two layers of skin off the palm of his hand, and he dropped to his knees on the elevator roof in silent agony.

The elevator was going up. It passed Jenny's floor and rose into the darkness. Slowly, shaking as it went, but inexorably.

Jesus, thought Johnny, *I must have shifted it loose when I walked across it, and even though Wheeler's called it down it still has to go right to the top before it can return.*

"Help!" he yelled. "For Christ's sake—I'm trapped on top of the elevator! Help! Dr. Ross! Help me!"

He heard Captain Barnes shout, "The relay box! Wheeler—for God's sake, where's the relay box?"

But then Johnny looked up and saw gears and pulleys and shining steel cable and he knew that nothing was going to happen in time to save him. The worst of his most terrifying nightmares came true as the dark space he was trapped in grew smaller and smaller until his hands reached up to stop the ceiling from crushing him, and all that happened was that the bones of his forearms were driven through the skin of his elbows and right through the wooden roof of the elevator car.

He didn't—or couldn't—scream. The air was pressed out of his rib cage in an odd, muted sigh, and then there was a crackling sound, like someone crumpling up a cellophane bag, as the bones in his body were broken. The elevator jerked, shuddered and stopped. Johnny's blood spilled over the edge of the roof and began to flow dark and crimson down the latticework gate, first down one diagonal and then down the next, making a zigzag pattern to the floor.

They brought the elevator down. Captain Barnes took one look at the crushed, birdlike figure on the roof, and said, "Call an ambulance, Wheeler. And make it fast."

Jenny St. Clair stood at her apartment door, just where Johnny had left her, her hand over her forehead as if she was suffering from a sudden headache. Then she heard footsteps coming up the stairs, and a familiar voice saying, "Captain Barnes? Is that you? What's going on here?"

"Oh, Peter," she sobbed. "Oh, Peter, thank God it's you."

26

THE SOUND OF the ambulance siren died away down the street outside. Captain Barnes stared out of the window balefully, watching it go. Behind him, sitting side by side on the flowery settee, Dr. Ross and Jenny watched him without saying a word. Sergeant Wheeler looked in for a moment, then said, "See you later, Captain," and closed the apartment door.

Jenny stood up. She was pale and she was still trembling. Dr. Ross said, "Here—" and handed her his jacket from the arm of the settee.

"I'm okay," she said. "It's just the shock. Can I offer you a drink, Captain Barnes, or aren't you allowed to booze on duty?"

"I'll pass, thanks," said Captain Barnes in his harsh, gravely voice.

Dr. Ross got up too, and walked across to the kitchen area. "I hope you don't mind if I do," he said.

Captain Barnes stared at him steadily. "You go ahead," he said. "You need it more than I do. After all, this boy's death was your responsibility."

"*My* responsibility? Who let him out of Lakeshore in the first place?"

"Come on, Doctor," snapped Captain Barnes, "you

knew he was coming here yet you didn't tell me. Don't you think that's a pretty blatant example of obstructing justice? If we'd have caught him in the street outside, then none of this would have happened. He'd still be alive now."

"You can guarantee that, can you?" asked Dr. Ross hotly. "You can guarantee that you wouldn't have found some other way of putting him to death, like shooting him in the back, or beating his brains out?"

"I can only guarantee one thing," retorted Captain Barnes. "I can guarantee that you and Miss St. Clair are both in a great deal of trouble. You knew there was an APB out on Venuti. You knew where he was. Yet you told him to come here and hide."

"He was frightened of you," insisted Dr. Ross. "I was worried that if he saw a police car, he might try the same kind of stunt as Henry Lawson. I thought that if he came here, I could drive him straight back to the hospital and get him locked up again without endangering his life."

Captain Barnes thrust his hands into his raincoat pockets. "Did you see the body?" he asked sharply.

Dr. Ross nodded.

"Well," said Captain Barnes, "next time you're worried that somebody's life may be endangered, do them a favor and stay away."

Dr. Ross poured himself a stiff Scotch and swallowed almost half of it in one gulp. "You've been on my back ever since I started this phobia program, Captain. If it hadn't been for you, and the hostility you've stirred up against it, the program might have been one of the most resounding successes in modern criminal psychology."

"Well, you're entitled to your opinion," said Captain Barnes. "But I'm entitled to mine too, and that is that psychotherapy doesn't have any place in a prison. Prisons are for punishment, and for rehabilitation by the oldest technique in the book—if you're released, and you commit another crime, then you're straight back in stir as fast as we can get you there."

"I'm glad to see that you're keeping yourself up-to-date on the latest criminological thinking," said Dr. Ross sarcastically. "Anyway, tell me—how did you know that Johnny Venuti was here?"

"Just a guess, that's all. He was spotted by a patrol car, walking south from Clark. The officers lost him in the crowds, but it occurred to me that he might be making his way to call on Miss St. Clair."

Dr. Ross said, "Well—I suppose that was good detective work." Although at the same time he was thinking, *Sergeant Wheeler promised he'd call off the APB for twenty minutes, and when Johnny was only a short distance from that telephone booth on Clark, the alert must still have been off—*

Captain Barnes pulled up the skirts of his raincoat and sat down in a basketwork chair. "You should soak this chair in water once in a while," he said. "Then it won't creak."

"Captain—" said Dr. Ross.

"I know what you're thinking, Doctor," interrupted Captain Barnes. "But Sergeant Wheeler told me all about your little conversation in the parking lot, and as a matter of fact he *didn't* call off the APB. That's why I guessed it was even more likely that Venuti might show up here."

"Henry Lawson talked to me, you know, before he fell."

"So what did he say? That he was frightened of us? Well, maybe he had good reason to be frightened of us. Maybe he was guilty of conspiracy to murder Barbara Grey by having somebody plant that bomb in your apartment. Do you seriously think after all the years I've put in for the Cleveland Police that anybody's

going to worry if I leaned on a convicted cop killer
a little?"

Dr. Ross slammed his whiskey glass down on the
kitchen counter. "That's the way you look at everything, isn't it?" he demanded. "You stick labels on
everything you come across. Henry Lawson happened
to shoot a policeman because of his phobia, and so
he's automatically a cop killer, a man without any
dignity or rights. I'm a quack headshrinker, as far as
you're concerned, and so I'm fair game for all of your
reactionary, back-biting criticisms. Jenny's a sculptor,
so I suppose that makes her a long-hair leftist intellec-
tual. Just let me ask you something, Captain Barnes,
when you've quite finished categorizing everything, what
the hell do you wind up with? You haven't made any
arrests, you don't know what's going on here any more
than anybody else. Intellectually, you're just a box of
gummed labels, looking for something to stick themselves on."

Captain Barnes smiled and shrugged. "What I've
been looking for," he said, "is a pattern."

"A pattern?" asked Jenny, frowning.

"That's right," said Captain Barnes. "You see, what
we have here is a series of fatalities occurring among a
very small and special group of people. And yet there
doesn't appear to be any consistency in the way that
they've died. There was Barbara Grey—killed by a
booby-trap explosion. There was Henry Lawson—who
fell from the top of a building. There was Laura Adams
—drowned, probably forcibly, in her bathtub. And
now there's Johnny Venuti, crushed to death in an
elevator shaft. Two of those deaths are pretty clearly
homicides. Two of them appear to be accidents. But
because the accidents happened to those two particular people, at this particular time, they don't statistically ring true. I'm always willing to admit the remote

possibility that Henry and Johnny and even Laura might have died by misfortune; but I don't really think so. I surmise that what we have here is a systematic killer at work. A killer who deliberately and purposely wishes to exterminate Dr. Ross' little therapy group, and even Dr. Ross himself."

"You still think the killer's after Peter?" asked Jenny.

Captain Barnes nodded. "I think it'll come to it, in time. Killing Peter will be the grand climax to the whole show."

"I suppose you're going to sit by and let that happen?" asked Dr. Ross. "I suppose you're even going to enjoy it? I mean, I agree with you about the rest of these killings. I do think they're all connected, and I do think we have to look for a pattern. But the question really is—what kind of a pattern? A pattern of family vengeance, against convicted killers? A pattern of professional jealousy, against a highly successful therapy program? Or a pattern of police disapproval?"

Captain Barnes's eyes scarcely flickered. "I hope you're not trying to implicate the police department," he said roughly.

"Maybe not the *whole* department," replied Dr. Ross.

Captain Barnes grinned and stood up. "I think you've got a bee in your wig about me, Dr. Ross. I think you should look around your own hospital, and around your own private life. Then perhaps you'll come across the kind of pattern you've been looking for."

Dr. Ross stared directly at Captain Barnes, but Captain Barnes didn't look away. Eventually Dr. Ross said, "Is that all you've got to say? Or do you have some more questions?"

"I only have one," said Captain Barnes. "How come you took so long to drive from the point where the mobile operator put Johnny Venuti's phone call through to you, to Miss St. Clair's apartment? By my reckoning, you should have made the journey at least five minutes more quickly."

Dr. Ross ran his hand through his hair in exasperation. "Captain Barnes," he said, "the day you and your fellow police officers stop harassing people like me, and concentrate on doing something useful, like regulating Cleveland's lousy rush hour traffic, *then* you can ask questions like that. Okay?"

Captain Barnes said, "Okay," in quite a mild tone. Then he turned to Jenny and said, "How long have you lived in this building?"

"Three years," she answered uncertainly.

"And does the elevator often play up this way?"

"Well, yes. It's very old."

"Do you happen to know why it jams?"

"Sure. It's the cables. They're always sticking on the pulleys. It isn't dangerous. It's just a nuisance."

"Was the elevator jammed this morning?"

"No, it wasn't. It was running okay."

Captain Barnes thought about that, and then took out a notebook and made a ponderous note in ballpen.

"All right," he said, folding the notebook away. "I guess I'll be seeing you both again soon, as usual."

Dr. Ross let out a short, testy breath. "Yes," he said. "I guess you will."

27

IT WAS ONLY just light when they drove down to the lake at Gordon Park, not far from the hospital, and went for a walk. The grass was a dead silver color, carpeted with dew, and the lake was as misty and wide as the waters that Hiawatha had paddled across on his last journey to the place of the gods. Dr. Ross turned up the collar of his jacket against the cold, and Jenny snuggled in close to him.

Somewhere out on the lake an invisible ship beat its way toward Toronto and called mournfully through the mist.

They walked in silence for almost ten minutes, and then they stood at last on the edge of the lake, while the sky gradually lightened above their heads, and another day began.

"That Captain Barnes—he worries me," said Jenny.

"He's a species of human file cabinet," said Dr. Ross. "You shouldn't let him upset you."

"But he's right, isn't he? There has to be some kind of a pattern to all these killings."

Dr. Ross rubbed his eyes. "Yes," he said. "I expect there does. But *I* don't know what it is, and *he* obviously doesn't know, and honest to God Jenny I'm tired of thinking about it and I'm tired of talking about it. Let's just walk for a while, and then go home."

"Not to my place, Peter. I couldn't face it. Not after—"

He put his arm round her. "All right. We'll get a room someplace. Just until you get your mind together."

"I keep seeing that poor boy's face and hearing his voice."

"I know. I know you do."

They walked along about a quarter-mile further, until they were standing on a small knoll overlooking the lakeshore. The mist was beginning to retreat now, and for the first time they could see spectral boats moving across the water. The lake looked like a breathed-on mirror.

"Did Johnny have any brothers or sisters?" asked Jenny.

"Unh-hunh. His mother was a young prostitute. She used to shut him for hours in the closet because she didn't want her tricks to get to see him."

"Poor Johnny. Then nobody cared that he died?"

Dr. Ross looked at her. *"You* cared."

"And you did?" she asked.

"Sure," he said. "I cared, too."

They started to walk back toward the car. "I always wished I had brothers or sisters," said Jenny. "What about you? Did you have any? You never talk about brothers or sisters."

Dr. Ross stooped forward and picked up a pebble without breaking his stride. He juggled it up and down in his hand for a while, and then he stretched his arm back and threw it far out into the lake. They heard the faint *plopp* over the sound of the waves washing onto the shore, but it was too misty for them to see the spray where it fell.

"I had a sister once, back in California," said Dr.

Ross. "She drowned when I was seven and she was five."

"How did it happen?" asked Jenny.

He shrugged. "At home, in our pool. One of the commonest causes of infant mortality in California. She fell into the deep end somehow, and I couldn't reach her in time."

"Peter, that's awful."

He looked away, out across the lake. "My parents took it pretty hard. I don't think my father was ever the same again. But they never said anything about it to me."

Jenny, thinking of Johnny Venuti and of Peter Ross's long-dead sister drowning in the family pool, gave a quick shiver.

"You cold?" asked Dr. Ross.

"Yes," she said. "A little."

He stopped and looked around him as if he'd forgotten something important. "I'm cold too," he told her. "Let's get back to the car."

28

THERE WAS A blue haze of cigarette smoke in Dr. Clegg's office when Dr. Ross walked in. He'd shaved and washed his teeth in the restroom in the Titus E. Frobisher wing, but he hadn't had time to change his shirt. He flung his file onto the desk, and sat down.

The others acknowledged his arrival with embarrassed nods, all except Captain Barnes, who stared at him openly. Dr. Clegg was sitting back in his buttoned leather chair, the early-morning sunlight shining on his white hair; while Dr. Clemens and Dr. Toland were sitting opposite, tense and quiet and plainly unhappy.

Dr. Clegg cleared his throat. "I'll have to get right to the point, Peter. We've supported your program through some pretty tragic and disastrous incidents over the past few days, but with young Venuti's death I'm afraid we're left with absolutely no choices whatsoever. The phobia program is finished. There will be no further experiments with The Box or with implosion therapy in this hospital."

Dr. Ross glanced at Captain Barnes. Barnes said nothing, but gave him a small, knowing smile. Dr. Ross thought, *You damned jackal. You look like everything you're not, but because you're a captain of detectives, nobody can ever prove it.*

Dr. Clegg said, "Considering how we met such a short time ago and pledged you our full support, Peter, it's necessary for me to say that we're all deeply sorry about the deaths of your patients, and that we regard what has happened to be a most unfortunate blow to your career and to criminal psychology in general."

Dr. Ross lowered his eyes and looked down at Dr. Clegg's rug. He'd never noticed before the way that Dr. Clegg's feet had worn a small oval patch just under his desk.

Dr. Alice Toland leaned forward in her chair. "Peter —I think I speak for all of us—we're just as disappointed as you are. I'm sure there'll be other opportunities, other grants, other hospitals—you'll be able to complete your phobia work one day—"

"And we're going to keep a very low profile on all of this," said Dr. Clegg. "You won't have anyone at Lakeshore giving you problems with adverse references, or anything of that kind. We still feel positive about you, Peter. I just hope you can understand our position."

Almost as if he hadn't been listening, Dr. Ross said, "Bubba's still sleeping. Did somebody tranquilize him last night?"

"I gave him a light medication," said Dr. Toland. "He should be awake by ten. The warden's sending a car down to pick him up at lunchtime. He'll be back in the state pen by this evening."

"I see," said Dr. Ross. "Well, if none of you object, I guess I'll go down to the wing and see if he's stirred yet."

Dr. Clegg said, "No more treatments, Peter. You're shut down."

"You made that perfectly clear, Dr. Clegg," said Dr. Ross, although he was looking at Captain Barnes all the time. "But you don't mind if I just say 'good morning' to him—and maybe 'goodbye'?"

"The press are all here," said Dr. Clegg. "Don't you want to join us?"

"No thanks," said Dr. Ross. "I'd rather say my farewells in a more intimate way."

He picked up his file, stood up and went to the door. Sergeant Wheeler was standing there, with a benign smile on his face. Dr. Ross paused for a moment, and then pushed his way past into the corridor.

He was almost at the doors of the Titus E. Frobisher wing when a voice called, "Peter—Peter, wait!"

He stopped. It was Dr. Alice Toland, hurrying after him from Dr. Clegg's office. She came up and stood in front of him, and her eyes were full of sympathy and concern. He knew it was sympathy and concern. He'd seen it all in her eyes before.

"Peter," she said, "I'm really so sorry."

He pulled a face. "You didn't have any choice, did you? And think of Barbara and Henry and Laura and Johnny. I guess they're feeling pretty sorry for themselves, too."

"You know what Captain Barnes says," Dr. Toland said, reaching out for his hand.

"Captain Barnes says a lot of things. You can't believe all of them."

"But he truly believes that the killings will stop if we announce the closure of the phobia program."

"Alice, there isn't anybody left to kill."

"There's Bernard King. And there's you."

He grunted. "I appreciate your anxiety for my safety. But, really, I can look after myself."

"Peter, I'm worried about you."

He released her hand and started to walk toward the phobia wing. She followed him, trying to keep up. "I appreciate your worry too. But I'm all right. I'm fine.

If anybody tries to bump me off, I have a gun in my
desk; and if anybody tries to impugn my medical reputation, I have a very good lawyer who specializes in
medical libel. Now, will you please leave me alone.
I want to see Bubba."

He pushed his way through the doors of the Frobisher wing, and left Dr. Toland standing outside. The
doors creaked backward and forward and finally came
to rest. Dr. Toland hesitated for a while, and then she
pushed them open herself, and began to walk briskly
along the corridor toward the security rooms where Dr.
Ross's phobia patients had been kept.

The security guard unlocked the steel door for her
and gave her a cheerful salute. "I'll be glad to be off
this job, I can tell you." He grinned. "Playing nurse-
maid to a whole bunch of fruitcakes."

Dr. Toland gave him a look of schoolmarmish disapproval. "The patients at Lakeshore," she said, "are
not fruitcakes."

"No ma'am," said the security guard, unabashed.

Dr. Toland walked along the corridor until she
reached Bubba's room. His bed was wrinkled and slept
in, but he was gone. She hesitated for a moment, and
then she walked along further until she came to the
door of the treatment room. She looked through the
circular window in the door, and she saw Peter sitting
there, beside his console, and Bubba hunched up on a
chair facing him. Peter was waving his hand and obviously talking to Bubba expressively.

Poor Peter, she thought. His whole world has just
come crashing in on him. Peter the proud, Peter the
progressive, Peter the piper who found he could no
longer call his own tunes. She smiled to herself as she
watched him, and then she turned away from the
window and walked back toward his office.

There, on his desk, was the photograph of his father.

Dr. Toland picked it up, looked at it and then set it down again. They had the same eyes, Peter and his father. She'd always thought that. She opened the middle drawer in the desk, and poked around to see if it contained anything interesting.

There were a box of paperclips, a six-inch rule, a half-eaten tube of Life Savers and a sheaf of newspaper cuttings. There were also a Smith & Wesson .38 safety revolver and a box of cartridges. Dr. Toland knew about the gun—Peter had bought it when the phobia program had first started, as a concession to all those friends who had warned him that working with convicted killers was going to be a dangerous business. She remembered what Peter had said. "I'm going to cure them, and then I'm going to blow their brains out?" But he'd still bought the gun.

Dr. Toland closed the drawer and walked across to the filing cabinet. The key was still dangling in it, and the top drawer was half-open. She slid the drawer out a short way and looked inside. There, on the identification tabs, were the names of Barbara Grey, Laura Adams, Henry Lawson, John Venuti. They stuck up like small pasteboard gravestones.

She picked Barbara Grey's file. Barbara had been the first to die. She lifted it out of the drawer and took it across to Peter's desk, where she sat down and spread the file out in front of her. There was everything here— prison photographs, police records, treatment graphs, vital responses, psychoanalytical tests, polygraph tests —everything. Dr. Toland brushed back her hair with her hand and started to read.

There was a sudden noise at the door. Surprised, she looked up. It was Jenny St. Clair, in a sculptor's smock and corduroy jeans. Jenny had raised her hand, as if she was about to knock at the open door, but she had obviously seen the picture of Peter's father on the desk and hesitated.

"I'm looking for Peter," she said. "I haven't got the wrong office, have I?"

Dr. Toland closed Barbara Grey's file. "No, this is Peter's office."

Jenny walked in, took off her shoulder bag and hung it over the back of a chair. "I didn't know you worked with Peter," she said, and there was an unmistakable challenge in her voice.

"I don't," said Dr. Toland.

"You're looking through his files," Jenny pointed out.

"Yes," said Dr. Toland. "I thought it might be a good idea."

"Without his permission?"

Dr. Toland shrugged. "Of course. He wouldn't have let me do it out of choice."

"So that's how his colleagues treat him, is it?" said Jenny. "He's just lost everything that means anything to him, and you pick through his papers to see if there's any other way to ruin his reputation."

"I think you've got it wrong," said Dr. Toland.

"Have I?" asked Jenny, bitterly. "Well, maybe you're the one who's got it wrong, Dr. Alice Toland. Maybe you're the one who's so eaten up with jealousy and vengeance that you'd do anything to tear Peter down."

"Anything? Meaning what?"

Jenny stared at Dr. Toland fiercely, and then turned away. "Meaning anything," she said, under her breath.

"Like murder? Like killing off his patients, so he doesn't have any program left? I hope you're joking."

Jenny tugged at her hair, embarrassed.

"Listen, Miss St. Clair," Dr. Toland continued, "you and I aren't enemies. Each of us is devoted to Peter, but in very different ways. I used to love him the way you do. Yes, I admit it. But I don't any longer. These days, I'm only interested in him as a close friend, and as a good person, and as a brilliant behavioral psychologist. You don't have any cause to be jealous of me, because I'm not jealous of you."

"Why were you searching through his files?" demanded Jenny.

"Stop bristling, will you?" said Dr. Toland. "What's happened in the past few days has been overwhelming . . . traumatic. . . . I thought I might discover some hint in Peter's files of why it all happened. He's been under so much stress himself that maybe he's overlooked some obvious, vital clue. After all, four out of five patients in this project are dead. Their deaths must link up somehow."

"You sound like Captain Barnes," said Jenny.

"Well, maybe I do. But Captain Barnes isn't a rookie, and maybe he knows exactly what he's looking for."

"Captain Barnes is just like all the rest of you. You've been sitting around like buzzards on the fence, licking your lips and waiting for this whole program to collapse."

"I didn't know that buzzards had lips," said Dr. Toland.

"I didn't know that senior psychoanalysts had the talents to burgle their colleague's files," retorted Jenny.

Dr. Toland stood up. "Listen," she said, "I've told you before and I'll tell you again. Dr. Clegg and Dr. Clemens and all the rest of the Ethics Committee have given Peter every possible assistance and every possible inch of rope. This hospital believed in the phobia program, and still does, but there isn't any way that Peter can continue with four out of five of his patients dead. The press are going to make ground beef out of him as it is."

"You mean he's completely finished here?" asked Jenny.

Dr. Toland nodded. "I'm afraid so. The committee met about twenty minutes ago and told him."

Jenny sat down. "I was afraid that was going to happen. I guess that was why I came over to see him."

"To comfort him?"

"To be with him, yes. I still think he's in danger."

Dr. Toland said, "Captain Barnes believes the immediate danger is over. Or at least it will be, when the press announces that the phobia program has been called off."

"So Captain Barnes thinks it's someone who doesn't like the idea of killers being mollycoddled?" asked Jenny.

"He thinks it's a possibility."

"And what about you?"

"I don't know," said Dr. Toland. "I was hoping these files might give me a clue."

"And have they?"

"I haven't had the chance to check through them yet."

Jenny took out a Pall Mall and lit it. She didn't smoke often, but right now she felt that she needed to. "Has Peter given you any ideas who might have done it?" she asked.

Dr. Toland shook her head. "Peter's been totally unresponsive about the whole thing. Very proud, very unassailable. But that was the way he always was."

"Maybe with you," said Jenny. "With me, he's always been warm."

"Well," said Dr. Toland, "perhaps that's the difference between you and me that makes Peter prefer you." Her voice was strained, but resigned.

"You should have heard him this morning," said Jenny. "He was telling me about his kid sister."

"I didn't know he had one," said Dr. Toland.

"She drowned in the family swimming pool when he was seven years old," Jenny explained. "Peter tried to save her, but he couldn't."

Dr. Toland looked at Jenny, and thoughtfully raised her hands to her cheeks. "That was why he was afraid of the water," she said.

"What?" asked Jenny.

"I said—that was why he was afraid of the water. He was always telling the Committee that his childhood fear of the water had been his inspiration for the phobia program. His father threw him in the deep end of the pool to teach him to swim—and that was how he formulated his implosion therapy. Facing up to your innermost fears by having everything thrown at you at once."

Jenny raised her eyes. "You're worried," she said. "What's the matter?"

"I don't know," said Dr. Toland. "It's just that if Peter's sister drowned in the pool, and Peter was unable to save her, then Peter might have interpreted his father's method of teaching him to swim as a punishment."

"I suppose that's possible," said Jenny. "After all, Peter said that his parents never discussed the drowning with him. He got the impression that it hit them pretty hard, but they never talked about it."

"Well, that would have made him feel even more guilty," Dr. Toland explained. "Unless you talk out a traumatic situation like that with a child, the child feels that he's somehow to blame. So when Peter's father suddenly upped and threw him in the pool—even though he probably did it because he was desperately anxious that the same thing shouldn't happen to both his children—Peter may have thought that his father blamed him and actually wanted to drown him."

"You mean—"

"I mean that Peter believed he was a failure. Because he hadn't been able to rescue his sister, he was a failure. And his father showed him that the only way to deal with failures is to . . ."

Jenny stood up. When she spoke, her voice sounded very shaky. "I hope you know what you're saying," she said.

"I hope I don't," Dr. Toland told her.

"You're wrong," said Jenny. "You must be wrong. You're only saying things like that because you're still jealous. Peter left you and you hate him for it."

Dr. Toland didn't answer. She didn't even appear to be listening. Instead, she picked up the phone and said, "Dr. Clegg?"

Jenny said, "What are you doing? You can't stir up any more trouble for Peter than he's already got. Or can you?"

Dr. Toland said, "Oh . . . Dr. Clegg's not back yet. No, I won't leave a message. He's still in the press conference? And do you happen to know if Captain Barnes is there too? All right. I'll go see him there."

Jenny tried to snatch Dr. Toland's arm as she left the room, but Dr. Toland shook herself free.

"If you think you're going to get away with this," said Jenny, "then you're reckoning without me, and without Peter, and without the U.S. Department of Health. By the time I'm finished with you, you won't even be able to find yourself a job analyzing urine samples, let alone patients."

"You can threaten what you like," said Dr. Toland. "I understand how you feel. But right now, I think there's something more important to consider than petty female jealousies, don't you? Peter's in the treatment room with Bubba King—I suggest you go in there and keep him occupied while I go get Dr. Clegg."

"You want me to do that?" asked Jenny. "On the

basis of some half-baked theory about Peter and his
father and his sister who drowned in the pool?"

Dr. Toland laid her hand on Jenny's shoulder. "If it's
all unfounded, then there won't be any harm done. But
if it isn't—well, you could save some lives. I won't be
long."

Dr. Toland walked quickly off down the corridor,
leaving Jenny standing by the door of the treatment
room. Jenny hesitated for a second or two, and then
stepped forward to the window. She could see Peter
sitting beside his console, and Bubba too, sitting in his
chair with his head down. Peter's hands were waving
emphatically as if he was explaining something to
Bubba.

Jenny turned around. The security guard was just
closing the door behind Dr. Toland, and the sound of
the seven-lever lock had a terrible finality about it. She
could understand why Peter's phobia patients had
fought so desperately hard to stay out of prison, and
that understanding frightened her even more than before. If they had all fought so hard to be cured, and yet
still failed to make the grade, that meant that it hadn't
been the patients who'd been at fault, but the whole of
Peter's phobia therapy program.

Maybe Captain Barnes had been right. What had he
said in her apartment? *"Killing Peter will be the grand
climax to the whole show."* He hadn't said *who* would
kill Peter, or why.

Cautiously, Jenny opened the door to the old lecture
hall. She stood there, only a foot or two into the room,
and let the door swing closed behind her on its oil-
filled hydraulic hinge. Bubba, on the other side of the
room, quite close to the untidy outline of The Box, sat
motionless, staring at the floor. Dr. Ross was lit only
by the telltale lights on his console.

"The problem is," Dr. Ross was saying, "you can't

find anyone to understand these days. You can't find anyone of sufficient intellect to grasp what you're trying to do, and how much money and time you need to do it. They give you the grant, and they give you the facilities, but they're waiting with their mouths full of saliva for you to fail. They *want* you to fail. They enjoy the spectacle of someone with brains and perception and talent being torn apart. Did you ever hear of the Roman games, Bubba? The way they used to throw the Christians to the lions? The way they used to train gladiators in all the skills of combat, just to watch them die? Well, nothing's changed. It's all the same today. They saw how promising I was, they saw how determined I was, and they all put their scheming heads together and decided that it was time to sacrifice me. They set me up, you know that? Dr. Clegg and Dr. Clemens and Alice Toland, with their smiles and their sympathy and their full support. And worst of all, that Captain Barnes. If you're talking about Roman games, then Captain Barnes has only one part to play. He's Emperor Nero, with his thumb permanently turned down."

Jenny said, "Peter?"

Dr. Ross looked around. "Jenny?" he said. "Is that you?"

"Peter—I heard what happened—I heard they closed the program—"

Dr. Ross stood up and came across the room. "Yes," he said. "Yes, they closed the program."

"Are you all right?" asked Jenny. "You seem—"

"I'm fine," he said. "I was just blowing off steam to Bubba here."

"You don't really think they set you up on purpose?"

He pulled a face. "What if they did? It's all turned out for the best."

"The best? But they closed you down."

"Sure. But I'm ready to move on now. There's no

doubt about it, I've outgrown Lakeshore. And five patients? How can I manage a full-scale therapy program with just five patients? I need at least twenty to get the results I'm expecting."

Jenny reached out for him, but somehow he managed to turn around so that she couldn't quite touch him.

"You seem . . . very calm," she said.

"I am," he told her. "I'm very calm indeed. I've been thinking about moving on, haven't I, Bubba? What do you think about Houston? Fine facilities there. Great hospitals and clinics, plenty of spare money for experimental psychology. . . . I'll continue my experiments and maybe lecture at some of the more important universities."

Jenny said, "Peter, I'm not sure. . . . Alice Toland thinks that—"

"Alice Toland? You're not still worried about Alice Toland? When we move to Texas, we won't even have to think about Alice Toland for one single second of one single day. We'll buy ourselves a house with plenty of land, and who knows," he said, mimicking a Texas accent, "we may even strike oil in our own back yard!"

Jenny laughed. "You're really okay, aren't you? You've gotten over it. Do you know something, when Alice Toland talked to me just now, she really made me feel that you were going crazy, or something like that."

"Crazy?" said Dr. Ross. "Alice Toland said I was crazy? What do you think about that, Bubba? Would you say I was crazy?"

Bubba didn't answer. Dr. Ross walked over to the West Indian's chair, and laid his hand on the back of it.

"If anybody ever wants any evidence of how crazy I'm not, they can look at Bubba," Dr. Ross told Jenny with fierce emphasis. "Bubba was so scared of snakes that he was paralyzed every time he saw one. He even killed a woman because she threw a tray of necklaces at him, and he thought they were snakes. But now . . . Bubba isn't scared of snakes at all. I threw him right in the deep end, and he's not afriad of anything."

Dr. Ross spun Bubba's chair and, without warning, Bubba pitched forward and fell face-first on the floor. Jenny jumped in fright, and stared at Bubba's body in horror.

"Peter," she whispered. "What's the matter with him? Is he—?"

Dr. Ross smiled. "Look over there," he said. "Right in the corner, by The Box."

Jenny, trembling, strained her eyes to see through the shadows. "Is that a *snake* there?" she said. "Is that real?"

"It's real all right," nodded Dr. Ross. "A Mississauga rattler. Very poisonous, very quick."

"You mean someone switched your snakes without you knowing?"

Dr. Ross walked toward her, with a frown on his face. "Switched my snakes?" he asked, as if he was genuinely puzzled.

"Well, you're not trying to tell me you let that rattle-snake loose on Bubba deliberately?" She swallowed, and then she said more weakly, "Are you?"

Dr. Ross turned and peered back into the gloom in the direction of the snake. "Yes," he said. "Of course I did."

"But, Peter—why?"

Dr. Ross looked stern. His expression reminded Jenny uncannily of the expression his father had adopted for the photograph on Dr. Ross' desk. Paternal, caring, but unbending. *I'm sorry, my boy, but you've got to take your punishment like a man. We don't care for failure in this family.*

"He had to be punished," said Dr. Ross.

"Punished?" asked Jenny. "Wasn't he being punished enough already? A life sentence for homicide, and a phobia he could scarcely control?"

"Ah, well, no, I don't think you understand," said Dr. Ross. "I gave him every opportunity to cure himself. I gave him the most technically sophisticated treatment that money could buy. I gave him my own talent too. My own therapy. And you know how highly regarded that is. Or *was,* before Dr. Clegg and all the rest of these boondock psychiatrists got at me."

"Peter," said Jenny, "you don't know what you're saying. You can't tell me that you actually killed all your patients yourself?"

"No, of course I didn't," said Dr. Ross, smiling at her. "I simply punished them. They refused to be cured, no matter what I did for them, and so I punished them. Look at Barbara. I sent her out for a walk, and I gave her two choices. Either complete your walk, I told her, and return to the hospital, or, if you panic, go around to my apartment. Well, she panicked, and failed, and that was why the booby trap was waiting for her. It wasn't murder. It was punishment. If she'd managed to finish her walk, and go back to the hospital, nothing would have happened to her at all. You can't call that murder."

"For God's sake, Peter," said Jenny, "tell me you're making this all up! For God's sake, tell me you're kidding me!"

Dr. Ross went across to the console and started switching off all the telltale lights.

"Then there was Henry," he said. "Poor, pathetic Henry. He was right on top of that building, scared out of his mind, and he trusted me. Well, he was right to trust me. Nobody else could have cured him. But he refused to let me cure him! So, all I had to do was put him to the test. I didn't kill him. Oh, no. I put him to the same test as Barbara. I said, 'Look down, Henry,' and he looked down, and lost his nerve, and fell. He deserved to die. You can't tell me he didn't. If he'd been cured, he would have reached out and caught my arms and I could have saved him."

"But Laura," whispered Jenny. "Don't tell me you drowned Laura."

"Of course. She felt defenseless and frightened. She had no reason to feel that way. I wasn't going to rape her, or hurt her. But she got hysterical with fear. She failed. And, believe me, Jenny, there's only one punishment for failure."

"Johnny?" she asked. "Him too?"

Dr. Ross switched off the last of the console lights. Now they were standing in darkness, except for the glimmer that penetrated the old lecture hall from the window in the door.

"That was one of the neatest, and the most appropriate," said Dr. Ross. "He called me, and said he was in trouble, and so I told him to go around to your place. I said that if the police came around, he should hide himself on top of the elevator. They'd never find him there, I told him. But what he didn't know was that I'd gotten to your apartment before him, only a few minutes before, and switched off the elevator at the relay box. Everybody in the building was so used to the elevator breaking down that they didn't think to check in the most obvious place. But I waited at the corner and, when I saw Barnes and Wheeler go in, I followed after them, and switched on the elevator again, and when they pressed the button to get it going, up it went —with Johnny on top. Fitting, don't you think, for a failed claustrophobia patient?"

Jenny stepped back toward the door. "Oh God, Peter," she said. "Oh God, you can't mean it."

"Mean it?" he snapped vexatiously. "What are you talking about? I knew months ago that these five crazies weren't going to make the course. I tried to cure them, God only knows, but they wouldn't respond. The more implosion therapy I gave them, the more frightened they got! As if they didn't have everything to gain, and everything to lose! Look at Bubba here—I showed him snakes and he turned to jelly—that's why I bought this rattler. He didn't even die of venom, he died of fright. The snake bit him again and again—they don't like to use up all of their venom at once—and he screamed like a baby—after all that treatment—after all the help I gave him—he screamed like a baby—"

"Peter," said Jenny, "I have to tell you that Dr. Toland's gone to fetch Captain Barnes. You can't get away with it."

Dr. Ross scratched the back of his neck, amused and thoughtful. "Well," he said, "it depends what you mean by getting away with it. The first thing we have to do is get away from this hospital."

"I'm not coming with you."

"Ah, but you have to," he said. He walked across to her, caught her at the door, and seized her arm. She tried to struggle, but he was very strong. It was the strength of unhinged determination, and of years of ice hockey.

"You're not really going to leave me, are you?" he said, as he pushed her through the doorway toward his office. "Not after all those good times we've had? I've failed once, I admit that. I've failed, and you're a great success. But you can forgive me for one failure, can't you? Or can't you?"

Jenny whimpered, "Please—"

Dr. Ross kept a hard grip on her arm as he went across to his desk, opened the middle drawer and took out his .38 revolver. He flipped the chamber open with one hand to make sure it was loaded, and then flipped it shut again. He tucked it into his belt and gave Jenny a quick, self-confident grin as he did so.

"Crazy, huh?" he asked her, and reached down to open the bottom left-hand drawer. From beneath a stack of plain typing paper and a folded map, he pulled a child's doll. It was faded and old—at least twenty years old—and its red dress looked as if it had been bleached. Maybe it had been left out in the sun, or dunked in a chlorinated swimming pool. Dr. Ross tucked it under his arm and then said, "Let's go."

Jenny said, "Where are you taking me?"

"Nowhere," said Dr. Ross. "Just smile at the security guard on your way out."

They passed through the steel door with a salute from the guard, and there was still no sign of Captain Barnes. They walked along the corridor, past the gloomy portrait of Titus E. Frobisher, and through the swing doors to the hospital lobby. Dr. Ross was walking fast now, and Jenny almost had to run to keep up with him.

She prayed that Captain Barnes would see them before they left the building.

But then they were crossing the parking lot, and they were only feet away from Dr. Ross's Porsche. Dr. Ross unlocked the car one-handed, pushed Jenny into the passenger seat and then climbed in himself.

"I'm not going to hurt you," he said in a curiously distant voice. "But if you try to yell out, or make a fuss, I'll stop you. I mean that."

He started the engine and pulled the Porsche out of the parking lot with a screech of tires. He drove through the entrance gate, turned right and headed toward Gordon Park, where they had walked that same morning, close to the lake. Jenny closed her eyes and said a silent prayer inside of her mind.

29

FROM THE PARK, she watched him swimming out across the lake. It was almost noon now, and the sun was high, but still misty. He swam strongly and evenly, like the athlete he was. His shoes and his coat lay on the Tarmac path, carefully folded. His car was parked a few hundred yards away, meticulously locked. He was that kind of a man.

He had warned her not to call the police, or draw the attention of passers-by. He still had the gun, held high out of the water in his left hand, and so she stayed where she was, on the same grassy knoll where they had talked at dawn, and held herself in her own arms. as if she was cold.

Soon, she could scarcely see him. Only his dark curly head bobbing above the waves of Lake Erie. She wouldn't have been able to know that he was treading water as he loosened Suzie's doll from his belt and kissed it; and she wouldn't have been able to hear him talking to himself in quick, breathless gasps.

"I'm sorry, Daddy. I'm sorry I couldn't save her. I'm so sorry."

There were tears in his eyes as he lifted his head above the surface of the water and slowly pushed the muzzle of the .38 into his mouth. He didn't pause for long. He pulled the trigger, and there was a loud, flat report, and from the shoreline Jenny saw a dark red spray rise into the air from the back of his head and shower across the waters of the lake.

Then, there was nothing at all. Just a cheap 1950s doll circling around and around on the surface, and a trace of blood.

Jenny stood where she was, shocked. Behind her, she heard a car pulling up, and she turned to see Captain Barnes and Sergeant Wheeler climbing out of their dark green Bonneville. Captain Barnes strode toward her across the grass as if she was a long-lost child, and he was her father.

"You were too late," she said.

Captain Barnes looked out toward the lake and bit at his thumbnail. "Yes," he admitted. "I guess I am. I guess I always was."